PEEP GAME

Original poetry, observations, and fiction

1997 – 2007

PEEP GAME

Original poetry, observations, and fiction

1997 – 2007

By

Adalberto McFarlane

NINE Nappy Publishing   Sacramento, CA

NINE Nappy Publishing
c/o NINE Nappy Entertainment
PO Box 15423
Sacramento, CA 95851-0423
http://www.ninenappy.com

ISBN: 978-0-6151-6438-0
Interior Illustrations: Copyright © 2007 Adalberto McFarlane dba HOTEP Studios, a division of NINE Nappy Entertainment
Printer: LuLu.com POD (http://www.lulu.com)

Acknowledgements

I "started" this book in 1997, while I was looking at some poems that I wrote for various women I used to date. The first, *Beautiful Black Woman*, started the creative ball rolling in 1990. As time went on, I kept on writing and thinking about certain events that was occurring around me at the time. When I came to California, I had just the poetry done, I had let one of my college professor's review it, and she encouraged me to keep on going. Therefore, I have three (3) chapters of my character Michael R. Sloane©. I hope that I can turn it into other creations in the immediate future. Currently, my friends and family have encouraged me to continue with my writing. Information can soon be obtained through my website http://www.ninenappy.com for all of my future projects and current ones.

All I wanted to do was incite thought and intelligent conversation. I want to thank my family, especially my mother Maria and grandmother Benilda, who gave me the energy of never to stop trying, my little sister Amanda Christina ("Shorty"), my friends Michael Richardson, "big" John Ringgold, the CEO of *Prelude to Independent Living, Inc.* who laughed at some of my writings, jokes, comments and other projects, Uumoiya Glass, Owner of Brownglass Records (http://www.brownglass.com), my writing partner and fellow artist in the film industry, Emmanuel Kinley and Ricardo Santos (http://www.richardsantos.com), two good people who are fabulous artists in their respective genres. Also, a great big thanks goes to the ladies of Carol's Books in Sacramento, CA—Kitty Porter and Sharon Wright, who allowed a new poet a place to speak these words and give needed advice, editing, criticism, encouragement, and all-around love.

Where Did We Go Wrong?

Where did we go wrong?

Was it when ancient Kemet was known as 'the light of the world' and 'the center of learning' and we allowed the Greeks to get three degrees of knowledge?
Was it when we allowed those to come in to conquer us and steal what we know, claiming it as theirs?
Did we go wrong when the European came to our lands, saying they want to trade, but in reality wanted slaves?
Was it when we betrayed brother Nat Turner when he rose up to claim freedom for himself and his people?

Where did we go wrong?

Where did we go off the path?
When did we stop being children of the sun?
When did we stop being masters of our lives?
When did we begin to be dogs for an uncaring master and his house?

Where did we go wrong?

Was it when we allowed them to deport Marcus Garvey, send Noble Drew Ali to jail to die, allow WEB DuBois and Booker T. Washington to constantly and publicly argue about the same goal?

Where and when did we go wrong?

When did grown men become little boys?
When did our beautiful women become whores?

Where did it all go wrong?

Why did we allow the murders of Medgar Evers, little Emmett Till, Malcolm X, Martin Luther King, Patrice Lumumba, Kwame Nkrumah, and a score of others go unanswered?
How can we look at each other and call each other brother and sister?
How can we look at ourselves in the mirror and claim to be proud of our heritage?
When we don't teach ourselves or our children about our heritage
Where did we go wrong?

When did we forget?
When did we get selective amnesia?
When did we lose our way?

Why do we settle for someone who says the things we want to hear,
but doesn't do what he says?
Why do we even vote?
Why didn't we do like Japan after World War II—close the doors, get
together, formulate a strategy, and then put it into effect?
Why did we have to talk so much bullshit during the "Black Power
Movement?"
Why couldn't we just start small and in our communities, and then
build our support structure?

I guess we're really American, huh? We want it now! We want it
today!

Where did we go wrong?

When did we forget and bury the legacy begun by those who fought
and died for our freedoms?
Why didn't we put Shirley Chisholm in the White House—and then
painted it black?
We let Jesse Jackson run—and he did—straight back to Chicago and
Operation PUSH for his own agenda
Will Obama really win? Does he even have a chance? Look to yourself
for the answer
But, realize this: This country will never allow an African or African-
American president to run this country, they'll take a Caucasian
woman first

Where are we going wrong?
What future does this generation have?
Do they even care about the future?

Where did we go wrong?

When did we falter?
When did we become bitches in the war to regain our place in the
human story?
Where did we really go wrong?

Table of Contents

Preface

I am an aspiring writer, artist, filmmaker, animator, and entrepreneur. This book is supposed to make me see if the writer part can be a reality. I do not have a clue if it would. I mean, I wrote the words that appear in this thing, but the overall reaction--I do not have a clue. Isn't that always the way? Here you are, sweating and writing whatever great novel or screenplay and just building up all kinds of scenarios inside your mind if this thing hits big. But the reality is that you really don't know! This writing is some serious stuff for me, let me tell you! I got a regular job right? A 9 to 5 piece and here I am, late at night writing this thing. I mean, what possessed me to even start on something like this, huh? Vanity? Nah, I ain't *never* really been that vain to tell you the truth. Money? Please, in the book publishing business, unless you are a famous writer already, any *real* money is going to take years to come across, where the art can sustain the creator (This, not likely as of yet). For love? Yeah, I guess so—love of the word, the feelings inside, the emotions that spew forth like volcanic lava, the passion of the idea, the strength of the whole damn thing. The sheer muscularity of these epic words as they crash inside you, over you, under you...and within you. Writing is power man; can you dig it?

Writing is catharsis, and it has helped me to understand where my feelings, hopes, worries, and dreams come from—right inside little ole me. Yep, that's where they all come from (cool, huh? And to think, no expensive psychologist crap for like, 500 bucks an hour!). I am influenced by a variety of people, some which are famous, some which are not. Famous poets such as the group of men collectively known as The Last Poets, Puerto Rican poet/playwright Miguel Pinero, James Baldwin, Malcolm X, Nikki Giovanni, Sonia Sanchez, man the list goes on and on...then there is my mom and my grandmother, who both taught me to keep on trying and never giving up until I can't try anymore (y'know persistence). The words and subjects included in this book are sometimes harsh, sometimes filled with love, hope, dreams, passions, anger, questions and quandaries, as well as expressing what we all may feel at one time or another.

E tú sabes?
Adalberto McFarlane
Sacramento, CA

PEEP GAME ONE
Message to the Brothers

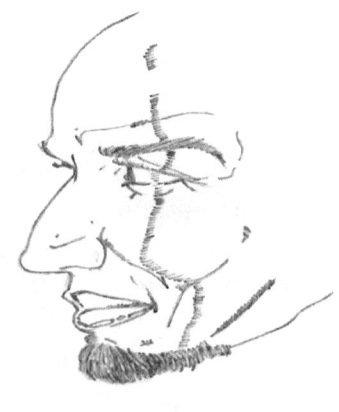

PEEP GAME brother, for this is one you've got to win. Check out the rulebook, for everything has changed since you came in. This game isn't new brother, its the still the same they've been playing on us since the slave days...only now, we're doing it to ourselves.

PEEP GAME:

    - Here *you* go: killing your family over a color

    - Here *you* is: trying to be a 'player and 'run game' on your sisters

    - Slanging rock in your house and 'hood; inflicting genocide upon the family.

    - Crying that the 'man is keeping you down - but its *YOU*!! **LOOK IN THE MIRROR**!

And see the real man who is *really* keeping you down!

PEEP GAME:

    - GENOCIDE

    - STRAIGHT MURDER

    - SLACKNESS

    - NO REAL KNOWLEDGE OF THE GAME

You're not a real "player" 'til you come correct in *all* arenas! Right now, you are still a trick being pimped by the game. Look at yourself: are you running shit *or* is shit running up into you?

PEEP the **GAME** brother, 'cause like I said: this is one you got to win -

NOW AND FOREVER!!

HOW DO YOU FEEL?

How do you feel?

I feel

Well, I feel like...

To tell the truth, sometimes I do not even know. Most times, if I am in a good mood, I'm happy or some state of content or 'normal' as if anyone has any idea of what normal is to man these days.

Especially to a BLACK MAN

Who feels like an animal trapped in a cage of stereotypes

Who feels like a house nigger, trying to fit in a world which 'smiles' at him

Who feels like a field nigger when I'm around my own kind, other brothers who know of this great weight upon our shoulders, and try to help each other deal with the responsibility of juggling two worlds.

Yes, I realize that this sounds absurd, with all of the 'progress' that we as a people achieved in this country, but the one thing that possibly cannot be changed due to upbringing (or home training) is as I said in the beginning:

STEREOTYPES

We all suffer from it. It's a damn shame, but Black folks got it worse than White folk.

Therefore, lets build up our communication, tolerance, and under/overstanding skills.

Okay?

FOR WE ARE HUMAN

BLACK

Spanish word is translated as *Negro*, a color. **NOT** an adjective!
According to *Webster's New World Dictionary*: "Opposite of white (in color);
dirty;(opposite of clean); evil (opposite of good), wicked (opposite of kind,
decent, etc.)"
The racist extreme is **NIGGER**
Your friend is your **NIGGA**
Your friend is your **DOG**
Your friend is your **BOY**
Your friends are your peeps...
Well peep this:
What you, me, all of us are is a mixture of different, amazing yet spectacular
race

FOR WE ARE HUMAN.

DA METHTICAL

Rolling up the paper...with the product of the earth inside.

Sealing it with the liquid flow off the tongue

Sparking the flame

Smell the burn

Inhale the sweet intoxicant...

Sit back - max and relax

Slowly now! Clear your mind!

Feel the smoke tickle your throat and enter your lungs

Notice the sparks it starts in your brain cells -

Now, it got you thinking...

Now, it got you analyzing...

Now, it got you hypothesizing on the abstract...

Now, it got you questioning the facts and figures

But you know what?

IT'S ALL GOOD!

Cause man: you're high!

Sittin' on cloud 1 9

And everythang's fine...

BUSTIN' CAPS

You're walking down the stairs. A look of death across your eyes, along with a dull haze of the bionic chronic swirling your brain. Your gat in the small of your back, ready at a moments notice. You go out the door - see your boyz waiting, passing the sack around like a bottle of Night Train. You get your hit and pile in; ya'll turning corners and drive up streets - cool as shit, calm as night...

"Somebody's gonna be gettin' smoked"

All you think. Gatz and pumps get loaded - cocked at the ready; the wait gets heavy, "There he iz."
The lights go off

"Waddup loc?"

The guns cough
Bullets penetrate the body, jerking it to and fro; then suddenly: LIFTOFF!!!
O'er the fence...he didn't even get a chance to run or scream
Hitting the gas - going, escaping fast
Ya'll laughin' - giving each other dap; proud of your accomplishment
But, you don't see, probably don't even care about
The mother, family crying...asking God **"WHY?"** clinging to each other for strength, for support. Wondering who to blame. But the only blame is toward two groups,
Two colors: Blue and Red - Crips and Bloods
Brothers, stop the violence and keep the truce.

Peace.

HERE *YOU* GO

HERE *YOU* GO:

Watching "The MACK", "Superfly" and "Murder was the Case" for what seems like the millionth time. You and your boyz - taking mental notes and watching the 'game' unfold. Afterwards, you play Too $hort...listening to stories of a cool ass pimp nigga called 'Shorty' while reading all the shit by Iceberg Slim and Donald Goines. When Ice Cube asks, "Who's the Mack?" All ya'll scream out: "ME!" Waving guns into the air.

At the jam, the DJ mixes 'Atomic Dog' and 'Freak Like Me' and all ya gangstas go wild, shaking ass and slinging pelvis like one wild roman orgy.

Outside a small bunch plays ci-lo and one talks big shit. All ya'll drunk and high as shit, laughing, losing and winning big money. A player gets mad - starts cursing and waving his gat at the others. Next, as you can guess: everybody's movin'and scurrying as shots ring out.

Music stops...everyone stops dancing
Someone screams, "Darren's got smoked!"

EVERYONE heads for the hills

Darren, lying there, staring up at the sky, a tear rolls out of the corner of his eye, blood drools out of the corner of his mouth. His last thought: "But, I just came to have fun..."
Rest in Peace

A POEM FOR THE UPRISINGS

Assuming all assumptions
Hypothesizing all hypothetical questions and equations
The unruly attitudes of the multiple servitudes
upon their hellish mannered masters,
wishing death and disease
upon neither either was they appeased

The flames flowed up and jumped about
Taking everything from a loving whisper to a horrified shout
The demons danced and the band played
While under covers and from behind locked doors, cowered the small-
thinking masters
With white eyes as bright as a full moon, they stared at the chaos - listened
to the melodies and witnessed change: swift, deadly with no remorse or
afterthought!
It was bloody, violent, hot and sweaty...
Barbaric in its tone - Quality was for naught; anarchy was the god of the
moment
And the masters watched
And the masters witnessed
With mouths gaping and gasping in utter disbelief
And they testified that what they saw was not only a one-time occurrence,
but the start of things to come!
Dedicated to: brother Nat Turner, Watts, Los Angeles, Detroit, Harlem, for
the spirit of the Million Man March, the Black Panther Party for Self Defense,
for all political prisoners, and for brother Mumia Abu Jamal.
Power to the people, As-salaam alaikum

A MAN CURSES

They say that a man curses because he has nothing else to express himself
with
Most men curse when angry; when an injustice has been committed
Most curse when affectionate toward one another, with words like
'muthafucka' or 'my nigga'
Some even curse out of ridicule while others do it out of habit
Also, we all know that it doesn't look *or* sound right when a woman curses;
most will agree, for it demeans her, pulls her to the lowest ebbs of the gutter
For men, it is hard to stop, since it comes so natural and we have been doing
it for so long...

So is cursing the same as gasoline: adding fuel to the fire?

DADDY, WHERE ARE YOU?

Daddy, where are you?
I miss you a whole lot
I miss your smile and your hearty laughter when you play with mommy and me
I miss your hugs and kisses. Even your comforting voice when I've been in a fight
I miss you daddy - momma's not the same: trying to be herself and you at the same time. I mean, we're alright -n everything, but it's not the same without you daddy.
I get funny looks from the old ladies across the street
And the other kids make fun of me
My teachers all think I'm a troublemaker
But that isn't true
Even the judge thinks so too.
The other prisoners call me 'bitch' and 'sweetheart' and claim my manhood late at night
I've had to kill to survive - even though you told me that violence doesn't solve everything
But I figure: I'm gonna be alright.
I'm in the chair while the priest says prayers for my soul
I'm clean, ready to go to my final place...all the while keeping in front of me your face

Daddy - where are you?

Maybe if you were here, I wouldn't be here...isn't that true?

PREPARE FOR THE REVOLUTION

Prepare for the revolution!

For it is coming

Prepare brothers and sisters, for it sweeps across like a smoldering blaze

Call out! Shout out!! Scream until your lungs burst and your breadth becomes shallow.

Prepare for the revolution: for it only comes once

The revolution will come at the same time as the judgment of ALLAH the Most High

We will see all the spirits of the past: brothers Marcus, Malcolm, Martin, Jesus, Muhammad, and Kwame...

When you see them, fall to your knees; cry that heavenly cry.

Junkies: wake up and quit that nod

Get off that pipe and sniffing that hit

Prepare for the revolution - for we will all be judged:

Jew, Muslim, Gentile, Christian, and Aryan - all of you will see!

Prepare for the revolution

Prepare for the bloodshed

Prepare for the flames

Prepare for the judgment!

Prepare for the revolution

For it will only come once

So - don't blink.

NIGGER-NIGGER-NIGGER

NIGGER - NIGGER - NIGGER!

My muthafuckin nigga!

I love you my nigga

Nigga, you my muthafucka!

PEEP this: Why do you love that word? Why do you love to say that word?

Why do you love to hear that word?

NIGGER - NIGGER - NIGGER!

Little black boy on the plantation, come here and take this disease out of my feet.

Lay your body under my soles and wait; wait like a good ole dog: obedient

NIGGER - NIGGER- NIGGER!

That is all you will ever be

A NIGGER: a stupid, lazy, ignorant creature

NIGGER - NIGGER - NIGGER!

Why do you love to associate yourself with that word?

Don't you know that it is a hateful word? A shameful word?

A word, which we shouldn't even speak out of our mouths

NIGGER - NIGGER - NIGGER!

Don't you know that it cripples and inflames our psyche?

It makes us react a certain way

It makes us act a certain way

It makes us think a certain way

NIGGER - NIGGER - NIGGER!

You look like me, you smell like me, you dress like me, you act like me, you talk like me, you *think* you are me

But I am not **you!**

NIGGER!

GET YOUR ASS OFF THE CORNER!

All you dope slangers, gangbangers, hanger-ons - why are you out here at all hours of the day and night, claiming you clockin dollars?
Get your ass off the corner!
Get your ass out of the 'hood if you're not going to contribute anything good. We have enough problems with welfare, social services, unwed mothers, deadbeat dads, sex offenders, child molesters and so-called prison reform...all of you say that you have "knowledge" or "street knowledge" as Ice Cube puts it...but to me, you don't understand the system as it fully works!

All of you might think you know the rules and the game - but the game comes upon us on so many levels

Get your ass off the corner!
Get your ass back in school!
Get your ass into the Schomburg Center!
What power do you think you *really* have? C'mon, tell me. Just because you have some police on your side, or fifty thousand guns at your back or any sexy black woman at your beck and call that you are the man? Brother Nimrod please! Haven't you realized it yet? **YOU HAVE NO POWER!** True power lies in the Mental, Physical and the Spiritual.

Let me manifest it for you:
The Mental: You might know how to turn a kilo of crack into a million dollars or know how many brothers you need for a heist...but in the grand scheme that will take you only so far. If you take your brain and study- and study hard on how Madam C.J. Walker, A.G. Gaston, and Reginald Lewis made their millions and don't forget to study the WHITE MAN - yes him, he got his eighty million and got thirty businesses all bringing him money; then you've

got power! Economic power that is! And in Amerikka: THAT'S FOR REAL POWER!!

The Physical: Is when you can take that Economic power and make things happen in and for your community - which will help it grow and prosper, like for example: building low-income housing or build a much needed daycare center, clinic or food supermarket.

The Spiritual: Which is the most important because of all of our beliefs, codes of honor, etc. The human will and determination has accomplished great and mighty works, which has either benefited or damned human beings.

Get your ass off the corner!
Get your ass and channel your spirit into something worthwhile!
Pick up a book and read it! Pick up the Holy Tablets; for the truth is there!!
Complete and uncompromising!

IT'S MORE THAN AFROS, DASHIKIS AND SLOGANS

It's more than Afros, dashikis and slogans!
It's more than a raised fist
It's more than an African medallion
It's more than quoting Malcolm X, Martin Luther King, or Huey P. Newton
It's more than listening to the Last Poets, Boogie Down Productions or Public
Enemy
It's more than reading "The Souls of Black Folks", Nikki Giovanni, Dr. Michael
Eric Dyson, Prof. Cornel West, or Africana: The African and African-American
Encyclopedia
What it is is having a code of honor, a way of life, a philosophy - a particular
system of ethics

The Japanese called it Budoshoshinshu - the warrior's primer; brother Bruce
Lee had it in his style of self defense: Jun Fan Jeet Kun Do; Huey P. Newton
and the Black Panther Party for Self Defense definitely had it!

A particular system of ethics
A system
A way of living
A belief

It's more than Afros, dashikis and slogans
It's about respect
Respect of yourself, your God, your lifestyle, your fellow man and woman,
your job and co-workers, your family, yours and others personal space

It's hard work maintaining respect
It's hard work giving respect
It's hard work even receiving respect

So let's all try a little harder, okay?

Respect each other
Love each other
Hug each other
Smile at each other
Shake hands
Shit - just laugh, dammit!!

Jonah the Poet

Standing on the corner, puffing on a cig
Stood a six foot tall nig named Jonah
Now to a whole lot of people, Jonah was a few things
He was a poet–but He didn't know it
Even though every word said out of his head
Was a rhyme and seemed to control time
He was a philosopher–spouting wisdom
From a wise dome that never earned a degree
Much less made it past grade number three

He was a warrior—defending his people whenever
The pigs came down too hard or without
Probable cause
Addict was another adjective to describe ole Jonah
He was addicted to life and all of its sweets, as well as the sours
He was addicted to that plant, that cheeba cheeba
That little green bud which would transport you to
Distant galaxies after a few puffs and if you didn't pass
He was addicted to wine—the sweet grape which grew on
The vine and when it hit his taste buds—He thought it
Was just so fine
For it kept him warm during the winter
Cool during the spring and summer
In the fall—it was the boss

Now he was preachin' and rappin' to the youngbloods
Who were wheeling and dealing the tricks of their trade
"You's already on lockdown clown.
When they catch you, you're going to jail

But I'm trying to school ya—cause in there's where you'll fail.
That place ain't made to learn from mistakes
Only to make more
And the more you'll make, the more they'll take
Till your time on earth is gone."
Now the youngbloods stopped and took a look
As Jonah was running his rhyme
They all knew and heard tales
Of how Jonah made it to the top
But the wrong turn down the wrong road
Made Him fail

One blood stood in his face
And copped his game
"Man, fuck you!"
And He pushed Jonah to the ground
But as He stumbled
He spit and mumbled
"You'll see—I can see your destiny."
Then his rear met the sidewalk
Just then, a car came round
Tires screeching, hands reaching
For guns hidden now revealed as shots are fired
And bullets were sent to do their master's
Bidding
Those youngbloods, well they got caught
Not by police but by rival bloods
Who were out for revenge
Jonah himself barely made it out alive
As the shots and smoke subside
And all He could see was the

Outlines of where the bloods had once
Stood and swore, joked, laughed, and talked.

PEEP GAME TWO

Message to the sisters

The women, our women...are telling us brothers that there are no good black men anymore anywhere!

The women all say that we are locked up in jail, chained on drugs: crack, marijuana, cocaine, PCP, homosexual, running to the white woman or punk ass niggas

Brothers **PEEP GAME**: What happened to make our women think like this? What have we done to make our women have this perception?

They say they want a brother, a man who will give them what they need - but what do they want from us?

Respect? Got to give it first

A man who will treat them right? Gotta come correct first

A man who will make them feel like a woman - make them feel wanted? What about our needs of feeling wanted?

Most women that we see from one point of view want a brother who drives that Mercedes Benz or the BMW with the spoiler kit; a man with the 'phat bank', one who can put her in the "lap of luxury" she swears she wants to be in!

But the other women in the other point of view can see a brother only for his money and what can he do for her!

Then there are the ones who are true to the game, the ones who can be a woman and let the man be the man - treat him with respect and she knows she will receive the same!

PEEP GAME brothers, the true men they don't see, the men who are fighting the odds - and beating them.

The true men who are raising our children - or helping our women raise them - like we are supposed to.

We, the true men who are striving to make this so-called "Amerikkan Dream" a reality - each and every day!!

BEAUTIFUL BLACK WOMAN

How many times can I look in your eyes and tell you that I love you?
How many times must I go to my knees and thank the ONE above who
created you? With an era of darkness behind and all around me, you are the
light at the end of my tunnel

I marvel you, for there is none that can compare to you

With eyes which has seen all...
With a voice which has said all...and has more to say
With a vision as you have - I mean your shape, the soft contours of each part
of your body
I say that the ONE above has truly did justice!
You are my blood: because you flow through me
You are my mind: because you know me
You are my skin: for we are the same...

In soul

In spirit

Through love, hate and other matters...I love you beautiful black woman!

For you are the queen ruling my kingdom.

YOUR SENSUAL SEXUALITY

My queen, let me praise your sensual sexuality

Please let me thank my Heavenly Father for such sweet brown chocolate as you
Your sensuality is charismatic. It rapes my five senses - it violates my third eye

Your sexuality is also an equal contender. The way it pulsates when your gorgeous, luscious brown thighs move when you walk! How your breasts, round and full, move with each step that you take - with every breadth you make

Your hourglass figure: so smooth - I could pour honey down your spine! I could kiss the innermost part of your thighs straight to your vortex

Those doeful eyes! That swan-like neck! Your bauble lips!

That bright red lipstick just makes me shake in my shoes when you pucker up

Oh, that smile! You show me heaven every time you do

Your sensual sexuality is unlike anything or anyone else

PRAISE GOD MOST HIGH!! Lord bless her mother and father for making such a fine specimen

MY EARTH, MY WISDOM

My earth, my wisdom - you make me want to rule the world you know that?
Every time I think of you, I believe I can
I look to you for support
I look to you for comfort
I will try to never say anything negative towards you
I will try to never raise a hand toward you
I will try to not ever let you down
I will be there to hold up the world on my shoulders so that you will not be
burdened with the weight

But, you will have to help me as well: I expect for you to let me be the man
and don't try to step into my cipher when you know you can't handle it

I expect respect because it is necessary
Respect I am due for I am trying to make it in this horrendous system
I expect trust throughout
I expect love unconditionally
My earth, my wisdom - I am a part of you
I am from you
I will honor you
I will cherish you
I love you.

MOMMA, PLEASE GIVE ME A HUG

Hey Momma,

You know I love you a lot, right? Then I hope what I have to tell you you will still love me. I have been your child for a long time...and I know that raising me has been no small task, with you being a single parent n all - but I think I turned out fine, all things considered.

Even though they say a man is supposed to be strong and isn't supposed to cry, but I forgot all that when I received the news. Momma, I know all about the precautions, but one time I forgot. In the heat of passion I was stupid - I've should've been smarter I know, but I wasn't and I'm sorry.

Please, let me finish at my own pace, for it is hard to tell you in this fashion.

I wish I could hold your hands - maybe it would have made it much easier. I've had so many dreams and plans, but like a raisin in the sun - they dried up and died.

Momma, this is really hard...Momma, please give me a hug; for your baby... is HIV positive.

I love you dearly,

Your baby

LADY, WHAT HAPPENED YOU (AFTER WE MET)?

England (June - July 1991)

Mildenhall AB at the Galaxy Club

Lady, what happened to you (after we met)? When I first saw you - you were so funny yet so beautiful. Now, to be honest, the dog in me was awake and barking when I saw you in that sexy red dress and those thick caramel thighs. But I felt something different every time we danced.

When we danced close and slow, you felt good. You felt like a missing piece of a puzzle - you fit right in. Now that I reminisce on our rendezvous, I regret that I didn't get your picture. I didn't get your name (if you told me, I forgot - sorry) or where you worked (I remembered that you were a nurse working at Lakenheath).

Lady, what happened to you (after we danced)? Why did you always have to run before the club closed? Acting like Cinderella at the stroke of midnight. But I was more puzzled when I returned the following year in April to see that you were not there.

And to this day as of this writing I still don't know who you are and all that I have are memories locked inside forever.

LORRAINE HANSBERRY, I LOVE YOU

I love you, Lorraine Hansberry, because, through Walter Lee Younger in "A Raisin in the Sun" you captured the Black Man's thoughts perfectly.

His dreams

His struggles - with himself and the world around him

And that dialogue that he says to George Murchison:

"And you? Ain't you got no bitterness - 'bout nothin? Don't you see no stars gleamin' nowhere that you ain't been able to reach out and grab? You happy? You contended little...Bitter? Man. I am a volcano! Bitter? I am a giant -   surrounded by ants! Ants who can't even understand what the giant is talking about."

Lorraine Hansberry, my sister I cherish you

I cherish you, because, you filtered through all of the filthy stereotypes and negative images of us - the Black Family

Sister - you are true!

True to yourself. True to us

"Dear sweet Lorraine" as brother James Baldwin called you out of affection

He was right. If you were alive right now sister, I would hug you and never let you go. I could do it

In my dreams

Through my woman

When I go to my ancestors

I will see you! And cry tears of joy for I love and respect you Lorraine Hansberry

Take care

MY SISTER...

My sister - how could you become this way?

My sister - how could you demean yourself this way?

My sister - how could you call yourself a bitch? A hoe? How could you become a prostitute? A crack-cocaine smoker? An unwed mother, living on welfare? A lesbian in prison? Demeaning me? Have nerve to deface me?

My sister - what is wrong with you? Is that mental chain that tight on your senses?

Don't you realize what I am doing for you? I'm trying to build a Heaven on this here Earth! I'm trying to build a Paradise in this land of despair!

But I can't do it while I'm in a jail cell. I can't do it strung out on crack

I can't do it living like a homosexual

I need your strength - just like you need mine. You need my strength to help you overcome all these walls. To break all these chains on your mental and physical self.

You know that you are not a bitch - so why are you acting like one?

You know that you are not a hoe - so why do you dress and act like one with every guy you meet?

Keep your legs closed!

You don't need to walk the streets selling your body. Walk to school and reclaim your life!

Come and claim ALLAH the Most High as you walk through these dirt roads. Take my hands so I can help you!

Take your lips from around that glass pipe. Put it down! Leave it alone! Go back to school; get a job. Stop living off the Government like a slave, like a prostitute.

Are you happy my sister? On the inside as well as the out? Think about it for a moment...I didn't think so. Take my hand sister. Lean on me sister

I will help you - you will help me; and **together** we will prosper!

I'm A Fanatic

Earth mother, goddess, wife, sister, daughter, girlfriend
So many titles, so many descriptions
Landlord almost gave me an eviction
Because I professed my love for you too loudly
You hit me like cocaine or even crack
Cause I'm a dope fiend for your love and affection
I've gone through too many doors
Walked far too many paths
Through it all, I've managed to laugh
Sleeping while I'm awake, awake while I'm sleeping
Dying while I'm living, living while I'm dying
My mind is a bottomless pit
My heart is the rock of Gibraltar
My love is a whisper, being carried on a windy step leaf
Penetrating your heart, penetrating your soul, penetrating your mind
Till you are punch drunk or just slightly tipsy
    So here we are my sweet, tripping on the light fantastic
    I am a fanatic
    For you.

PEEP GAME THREE

Poems and Observations of Society

It's all a game right? Just like Monopoly. Just like Three Card Monty. Just like Ci-Lo. You always have it: the victim and the con man. The sheep and the fox.

The people and the Government. Don't you get it yet? The Government doesn't give a damn about you! They are making more money and getting wealthy keeping you downtrodden and dependent upon him more than you think you know.

PEEP GAME:

The Government sponsors all this drug trafficking into the country! The Government sponsors by keeping all of us from achieving our dreams. By piss poor education, low salary wages for teachers, not enough special education programs for children who really need them. The Government sponsors the war on the Black Family. They brainwashed our way of thinking. Kidnapped us and raped our beautiful sisters and took our manhood!

The Government put us all in these ghettos, the projects. Made the Black Family dependent upon welfare, drugs, and watch as we act like crabs in a barrel - pulling down anyone who is trying to get out and make a better life for themselves.

It's the Government who sponsors the poisonous products! They sponsor the infection of our people - they give us AIDS, Syphilis, a white Jesus as God the Most High to worship and only ALLAH the Most High knows what else! The Dragon is amongst us! His seven heads are looking everywhere at everything all at once. His claws are grabbing everything that isn't his and claiming that it is his. His teeth are biting and sucking out the blood of the Black Family like a vampire!

PEEP GAME: It comes in many different flavors.

PROTECT YOUR NECK (WATCH YOUR BACK)!

As I walk up to the microphone and look out among the faces and the shining, bright spotlights, I take a deep breath through my nostrils and let it come out slow and long. My hand pulls the stool up to the mic, I sit and then...then I begin:

Protect your neck (watch your back)!!
For the shimmering blade cuts it with silken ease
Feel the blood pour out like Kool-Aid from the pitcher
See it make stains upon that new white shirt
See the hands grasp and try to stop the flow
See the legs hobble and bend, the feet shuffle and grate against the hard concrete!
Protect your neck (watch your back)!!
The vultures encircle round the still living corpse steadily plucking still warm flesh from it
The Reaper stands and counts the seconds
The minutes
The hours
The days
The weeks
The months
The years
The decades
The centuries
The millenniums!
Damn!! It took a long time, it thinks
Watch its scale tip back and forth ever so slowly
Its hooded head blowing in the wind. Eyes are watching...
Recording

Remembering

Cataloguing

Protect your neck (watch your back)!!

Feel the bones and vertebrae break with each twist

Watch the head spin 360 degrees round as an owl does

See the spine bend in a half moon crescent as a rubber tree branch does

Damn!! Why did you fuck up like you did?

You didn't have to die!

But you did

Protect your soul (watch your spirit)!!

Preserve your life. Live your life. Love your life - it's the only one you have

in this world

Cherish every day! Live it like it's the last

The last day

Hour

Minute

Second

Cherish it.

PALEFACE SPEAKS WITH FORKED TONGUE

"Paleface speaks with forked tongue"

Isn't that an old Native American saying?

Do you understand what they meant by that phrase?

Do you even comprehend the meaning behind it?

I guess not...look at you: sitting here looking all confused and dazed

It's simple really: the white man is a liar! He's the biggest liar in the whole world!

The white man is the Government...he says one thing or many things, promises so many promises but he just goes the opposite way!

Doing one thing or other things, breaking all of the promises and deals that he gave his word on.

Don't believe a word that they say

Watch what they do

Read on what they have done

The evils that they have committed - the murders, the rapes against men, women and even against children

They are the biggest pimps

They are the biggest drug dealers

They are the biggest murders

They are the biggest con men

There he is: ole Willie the Lynch!

Get a rope!

DO AS YOU SAY NOT SAY AS YOU DO

Why is it that when we hear what a politrickain is going to do on election year that old saying still rings true?
"Do as I say not say as I do"
Why does these miscreants promise the citizens everything but deliver nothing?
"Do as you say not say as you do " indeed
Why can't all of you tricksters and hucksters just tell the truth?
Why can't all of you preachers just tell the truth?
Why can't teachers just teach the truth?
Because no one would believe it!!
The citizens have been fed propaganda for so long that the truth will sound just like another lie!
No one would care for you!
"Do as you say..." Fuck you!
I have never voted for any of you fake politrickians! Simply because none of you truly represent me!
So, do as I say... and suck these nutz!

WHO IS TRULY REPRESENTING? (IN MY OPINION)

Let me ask a everyone a question
It's a simple question
"Who is truly representing?"
Who is truly the description of what we all need in a leader? Someone to represent all of us!
Bill Clinton? Nope. Not even. The only thing Bill's representing is how much punai he can pop before they impeach him!
Hilary Clinton? I bet she's getting her share of the Secret Service Agents
Newt Gengrich? What kind of a name is 'Newt'? Isn't that a bug or something to do with a witch's spell? He looks like Jim Baker twin brother to me. He might be a closet homosexual, male intern popping guy himself!
Minister Farrakhan? Louis, you're not the Honorable Elijah Muhammad. You can talk a good game, but isn't it gettin old? "The white man's the devil...etc." Louis, what about the black devil? Where is the money from the Million Man March? In your pocket? Nation of Islam indeed - how can you have a nation if you don't own any land? Isn't that what the Honorable Elijah Muhammad said in his many books and in "Muhammad Speaks"? So did brother Malcolm. I agree with you on your ideas of self-determination, but your rhetoric of "The white man..." is old. Get a new script brother or read the books again!
Colin Powell? For president? Are you kidding? I didn't see anywhere what he did for African Americans during his time in the military or beyond. Did he help brother Malcolm with the OAAU? The Black Panthers with their school lunch programs? Someone find me his autobiography! If he did, I apologize posthaste.
Michael Jordan? Don't forget everyone who paved the road for Michael to do all the things that he has done: Earl Monroe, Dr. Julius Erving, Kareem Abdul Jabbar, and the mighty Wilt Chamberlain to name a few. The *best* thing that Michael is representing is that through education and sports, any other

obstacle is penetrable. Just look at history.

Who is truly "representing"?

Not the Declaration of Independence

Not the Constitution

Not the Emancipation Proclamation

If these documents truly represented the beliefs that were written on them, in my opinion, there would have been no slavery, Native Americans forced to live on reservations (which were old forts and raped land), no ghettos or poor people, etc. Everyone forgets: the so-called "founding fathers" were all slave owners! Just as 'ROOTS' showed, every time a slave was purchased they gave him/her their new masters last name! So stop debating on Thomas Jefferson's African American grandchildren. With slaves on his plantation and having 'bed-wenches' for sexual pleasure, of course they're related! Will someone stop this bullshit? Enough is enough!

Wake up and question the educational system!

If it was truly representing, in my opinion, there wouldn't be any teen pregnancies, or financial troubles because it should be a course taught in school.

What is there to represent?

In the words of Malachi Z. York: Right Knowledge, Right Common Sense, Right Wisdom, and Right Reasoning.

WHAT ARE YOU DOING AFTER YOU'VE MARCHED ON WASHINGTON?
(MESSAGE TO ALL THE MILLION MAN MARCH BROTHERS)

Brothers, on October 16, 1995, one plus million Black and African men and their sons stood in Washington DC and pledged to do right for themselves, their families and their communities. Money was collected that day from everyone. And money I believe was donated from those of us who watched on television - where is it? What happened to it? What did Louis Farrakhan, the Nation of Islam, the NAACP and the Rainbow Coalition do with all the money? Split it amongst themselves? What has all those brothers and speakers done since then? It's been four years now, the millennium is almost upon us and I got questions - I want answers! Here I was, a black man in America - ready to help my brothers do what we have been ready to do: come correct. But what happened? I didn't see a nationwide change go down. I know Mayor Guliani in New York stopped the "cleanup" Louis proposed to do at all the crack houses but there was much more to be done besides that. I saw a big rally and everyone went home to go on like business as usual; like all that love and promising was just because they were on television. I believed in the Million Man March!

Why is the Black Family still struggling? And just for clarification when I say the Black Family, I am talking about all those that are not Caucasian European American. What are you doing? Are you helping to build day care centers, clinics, housing or supermarkets or taking care of the elders? Getting rid of crime and drugs? Keeping tabs on the police and the politicians? Speaking out, expressing your opinions in an educational and researched manner? Seeing that any money you donate goes to exactly it is intended for?

What are you doing after you've marched on Washington? Me? I'm getting my life on track and coming correct with those who come correct with me.

IT TOOK YOU LONG ENOUGH!

"It took you long enough" was supposed to be about the NAACP under the leadership of Dr. Benjamin Chavis and the Nation of Islam under Minister Louis Farrakhan when they finally came together, squashed differences and with the Rainbow Coalition, joined to bring about the Million Man March on October 16, 1995. But now, after writing the previous essay, that I cannot write about two organizations in which I really don't believe in anymore. I have to question myself first and foremost, have they really made an impact upon me and my family and community?

I mean, once you get past all of the bullshit, sounding good, ego stroking rhetoric, and face the reality of your surroundings, what have they accomplished for the Black Family? Even though the NAACP have won some major battles in segregation but as a whole - what about the war? From a military viewpoint: which is better? Winning some battles or the whole war irregardless of the casualties? You have men and women who are ready to literally lay their life down for freedom in all of its forms.

To take the example of brother Malcolm X aka Malik El Hajj Shabazz, he was ready to die for freedom. The reason why I say this is because he wanted a better life for his family! That is where it all starts!

His family was his grounding base as well as his religious beliefs for a backbone. That was where he got his strength!

Think about it.

CAN'T WE SEE...

Opened the newspaper and saw the front page
It said that they've allocated $10 billion for new prisons
$10 billion...for new jails?
What are you trying to tell me?
What is it that I'm missing?
Can't we see that they are saying forget school!
Prison is going to be the place to be
Prison is going to be the new college
It is already! Don't believe me?

PEEP GAME:

The felons who are in for life are getting law degrees and PhDs!
What the hell is this?!?
How is this possible?
Can't we see that the prison system is where they want to send all of the African-Americans, Latinos, and ghetto folks who don't go along with their plans, who are not getting their shit together and get some kind of education to be able to deal with society, instead of being like a dumb pig in shit – happy in its ignorance and station in life.

Can't we see
Can't we open our eyes
And see that this isn't the way to be...

THE ROAD TO SALVATION

The road to salvation is a confusing map which does not tell you to "start here"

It is a long journey on a short path

It will present many images – which will be only mirages

There may be no signs to direct you

Or no mentor/guide to assist you

Some think that the road is paved with gold and other baubles, but they are mistaken. The road is harsh and hard, with many obstacles to bar your journey; to prevent you from reaching your desired goal – just like life or the life you lead.

The road is not made with green money – that false idol of security with images of deceased slave owners on them

The road is your own personal journey to discover your truths

It is made inside of you

Inside your soul (mind)

Inside your heart (spirit)

The journey may take many lifetimes to complete

Lives may be sacrificed

Hearts may be broken

No matter if its man, woman, or child

It is a hard journey – but one we all need to do

MISCELLANEOUS POEMS

Misc. #1.

Universal greetings when we be meeting:
    Hotep, Asalaam Alaikum, Rhaahubatt.
    Gotta keep changing, gotta keep shaking
    my mind is my own. My soul you don't own.
    No dead presidents worthy of my sentiments
    you deface me, disgrace me on TV. Claim you don't need me.
    but here you are copying me; with Canon copiers and corporate
    marketers, you smile your pearly whites while I light my blunt
    for the long, quiet night.
    HIStory - his story. I'm not down with his dogma.
    The Bible - is full of babble.
    The Koran - like a con, did the deed and ran...
    as fast as he can to Egypt.
    Picked it up and moved it to Saudia Arabia - yes!
    Saudi raped her, took her virginity
    took her femininity.
Call me nigger, Negro, Afro-American, African-American.
    So many names to confuse me; to describe me.
    But it's false. They're just adjectives - descriptions
    disgusting criptions to make me self-hate, beg & scrape
    But I refuse! Take their tools and recycle and reuse.
    Conscience knowledge with forethought; reading,
    meditating, self-taught.
    Poetry - tales of MY story
    My mother is Isis - Aset of Kemet.
    And I'm in the seventh heaven; her womb
    where peace & love reigns
    Peace...until the blood stains
    and screams of rage cover the air as a sponge covers my hair
    I look up in regal respect...sucking on her breast; which gives me
    strength. Strength of Gods of old and Gods of new.
    From polytheism to monotheism
    "Novus Ordo Seclorum" "New Order World"
    watch it unfurl

watch it unfurl
in time, time, infinite time.
The true constant
The ONLY constant that stays true.
True to the Holy Trinity—Aset, Usir and Heru
Transporting me through infinity
Time takes me to places I've seen only in my dreams
Dreams, which transforms into reality
Seeing that my story is not a fallacy!
Time, bringing me into today
Into tomorrow
Into forever, taking hold of me and sending me back to the past
To learn at the feet of I-M-Hotep
Transforming me
Telling me that my energy, is part of the All…
And the All is a part of me.

Misc. #2.

How long have we known each other? Months? It seems like years...
It seems like I knew you before...
How can I maintain my composure when I see you?
Everytime you smile when we talk or when I say something witty.
My heart skips a beat in your presence. As that long summer dress covers
your beautiful figure; hides that which men will kill for: soft, golden skin,
silky dark satin hair, bright brown eyes that shine like the eye of Horus. A
voice that brings heaven to my ears...
You send me for a spin! Ever since that first time our eyes first met; when
you wore your uniform--I experienced it then: your sensuality, your
sexuality that only a woman unto yourself can only display...

With confidence which makes mere mortal men shudder like skeletons in
their graves. Your attitude is an aphrodisiac! Setting my energies on fire.
But alas, these feelings must go unsated and unabated...my attraction to you
must go unappreciated...
For if we met at a different lifetime, a different place, maybe...
For now I must resign myself to a lesser position of quiet strength
For now I must resign myself to only one place...
As well as resign you to it as well inside of me
Since fate herself deemed it not to be
For thee and me will always be
In this lifetime and forevermore

Friends.

Stay beautiful

Misc. #3

I sit and write for a spell

Viewing out the window for no reason

Watching the seasons change

From white to green to yellow to brown

My town is my home

The world is my house

As well as my heaven

Misc. #4

I hear the witch's cackling laugh

Knowing it is my grandmother enjoying herself

Enjoying life

Pouring it all in a glass

Mixed with scotch and ice

With a Marlboro cigarette for a chaser

Misc. #5

Faulkner, Wilde, Salinger, Melville

Writers great

Writer of books

Great books these men have written

When shall my turn be?

When shall the spotlight shine upon me?

When next I look up, when will I have written a great book and become a

great writer?

Walking Through the Belly of the Beast

A Michael R. Sloane ©&® Adventure

Prologue

Our story opens in a metropolitan city, Washington DC to be exact. At the police precinct, where we see various uniformed policemen and others getting into riot gear and preparing for a major raid. The target: the Church of the Newborn Legion, an organization linked to rumors of child endangerment and abuse. Officer Michael Sloane is the head of the investigation as well as the leader of the team going in; meanwhile, another precinct is helping out with extra manpower, crowd control, and watching out for the press.

A phone call is made from the church to a covert agency – the Special Operations Organization, which is supposed to be part of Homeland Security according to official records. The voice in the office gives orders and warnings. The priest at the church assures his listener of no worries and that his defenses are preparing for the police right this very moment. Sharpshooters take their places at various windows to spy their quarry, all of them communicating through mobile devices. The sun shines through the clouds as they see the SWAT trucks and police cars arrive to block the area from bystanders.

Sloane prepares his men, a three-man team consisting of himself, Detective Max Snell, and Sergeant Williams. Sloane walks towards the rear of the SWAT truck and pulls out a necklace and opens it. Inside is a picture of his fiancée. He smiles and kisses it and puts it back under his uniform. Max Snell walks up behind him, "You ready, kid?" Sloane nods and they proceed to the doors. A second team plays diversion, but the sharpshooters begin firing to deter their objective. Two officers are hit while Sloane and his team make it to the doors, which are the main entranceway into the building. Behind them policemen is returning fire and the wounded being dragged out of the line of fire.

"Damn snipers! Fucking hate them. Looks like this ain't gonna be easy, kid." Snell says to Sloane, who is crouched against the wall, "It never is Max. This is really a hard one: we gotta get in their, save the kids and stop whatever ceremony their doing with them; a sensitive snatch and grab." Snell picks the locks, but to no avail. He pulls out a phosphorus pack to burn and melt the locks, "Entry in about a minute! Watch your eyes." He lights it and then a small, muffled 'boom' is heard. When they look, the door is ajar. They rise up and prepare to go in, "Watch yourselves, we got children to watch out for." Sloane goes to his team, "No shit." Snell responds. The interior is dark, light shines in from outside through the stained glass windows above. Their eyes catch the various wall etchings and statues, which align the foyer and entryway. Williams tosses a smoke bomb to cover their positions as they proceed. "Radio silence from here on out." Sloane goes. He recons an adjoining room and finding nothing, moves on. Snell finds a priest's room and spies a large mask of an Egiptian deity, "Freaks all around this place." Snell says to himself as he continues towards their target room: the main assembly hall.

In the dim light and smoke, Snell catches the glint of metal above them. "Sloane, duck! Three o'clock!" Snell yells out to the void. Everyone hits the floor and crawls forward, but random shots are heard coming from the hidden sniper. Sloane crab walks towards the shots, keeping his vision focused on the muzzle flash. When he is close, he lets off a few rounds in retaliation and changes his position to avoid return fire. When the smoke clears and the room is brighter, the sniper has Sloane in his sights and fires in rapid succession. Sloane rolls and maneuvers on the floor to avoid the rounds. He hears Snell and Williams returning cover fire for Sloane to run for cover. "Gotta get this guy!" Sloane says to himself. He turns back to the sniper and sends a few rounds his way; while the sniper sends a few of his own and hits Sloane in the thigh; while Sloane's rounds hit their intended target. The sniper falls off his perch to the floor below with a loud thud. As Snell and Williams approach Sloane, Snell sees a hand falling and releasing a grenade. "Hell no!" Snell kicks the grenade back to the dead sniper and jumps on top of Sloane, "Max, you crazy son of bitch!" Sloane yells as the grenade goes off, sending body parts everywhere.

"You alright, kid? How about you Will?" Snell goes to his teammates, "I'm fine. It went in and out." "Yes Base Command, we're alright...one man hit, not critical, sniper deceased. Gofer Team continuing further." Williams says to the SWAT commander in charge as Snell bandages Sloane's wound. When they reach the assembly hall, Sloane peers through the doors and curtains; what he sees he cannot believe: the church leader or head priest, Prince Muhammad, preparing to sacrifice a young African-American girl. When the men enter the hall, they see various worshipers, all young teens and older teens. The priest is garbed in what looks like ancient Egiptian regalia, chanting ancient words and incantations. They see that the young girl is chained to the altar, trying to wring the gag from her mouth when she spies the policemen in the rear of the hall. As Sloane proceeds to move forward, two very large guards bar their way, "No one enters the hall while the ceremony is in progress."

"Look cookie, that girl is about to be murdered! Let us through!" Snell yells at them, but they are like stone and do not move. Sloane looks at his team and then at the guards, "Sorry, fellas." Sloane puts his knee into the stomach area of the nearest guard, who goes down after losing his air by the surprise attack. The second guard tries to hit Sloane with his staff, but Sloane does a spinning back kick that shatters the staff and sends him to the floor. When he tries to get back up, Snell puts his weapon in the guard's face, "Have a seat, kid." The guard does as he's told. Snell and Williams and the sitting guard just watch Sloane literally abuse the first guard, who is now on his back, trying to prevent Sloane, who is on top of him, from delivering a serious punch to his face, "You win, I concede defeat!" "Smart decision." Sloane says as he rises and begins to run down the aisle towards the altar. Midway to his destination, a group of the children bar his way, "Damnit! I gotta get to that altar!" He tries to go around them and climb over pews; out of the corner of his eye, he spies Snell and Williams creeping towards the same goal. The chanting of the children begins to affect the officers; Sloane begins to get sleepy until he smacks himself and immediately places earplugs in his ears to block out the chanting, at the same time, he radios Snell, "Max, earplugs now!" "Roger." As soon as he puts his in, He sees that its too late for Williams, who is asleep on the floor, "Shit, one down." Snell looks for Sloane, who is still prevented by the children. He looks at the altar, at the young girl who is now yelling for them to help. Snell makes a decision, he draws his Glock and aims, "Freeze! This is the police, put down the knife and back away from the girl – now!" A dangerous laugh escapes from the priest, as he gives him a cursory glance and raises the knife to strike, but Snell lets off a few rounds, praying they find their mark.

The rounds hit their intended target; the children stop chanting and turn towards the altar, they see their leader twisting and jerking from the impact and he falls behind the altar. Sloane notices that the children look like they're awakening from a dream. He runs to the altar, draws his Glock and shoots the chains apart, as well as wrapping her in a tunic, "Its okay now. You're safe...he's dead..." Snell awakes Williams and they both carefully approach Sloane and the girl, who is resting in his arms, crying, "H-How is she? Is she okay, kid?" Snell asks. "Fine, I think." Sloane answers as he strokes her hair.

Just then, choked forced sounds are heard coming from Prince Muhammad. Sloane passes the victim to Williams as he and Snell go investigate. Sloane carefully motions towards him as he and Snell keep their weapons aimed in the priest's direction. When they come upon him, blood is everywhere, Muhammad is coughing up even more –he realizes that he is dying, so he motions for Sloane to come closer. The two policemen look at each other in bewilderment and then Sloane crouches down to hear what Muhammad has to say, he asks: "What? Last Rites? I don't have my Book of Coming Forth by Day and Night, sorry...but this should do..." He makes the sign of the cross over Muhammad and says, "Dominus Ominus, you'll be alright." As he begins to rise, Prince Muhammad's hand clenches Sloane's wrist, pulling him back down. Now Sloane listens with intent, Muhammad begins through spurting blood, "Y-You've been fooled I-little b-brother...you are nothing to him...a toy...you are a pawn in a very large chess game...k-know the players and the s-stakes...you may have a chance of stop-p-ping him..." "Against who? Who's in charge?" Sloane asks "C-Cassidy. D-Derek Cassidy. He has enacted an e-extermination agenda f-for America. Look for the other c-chess pieces..." "Who else?" Sloane asks again as he spies a red dot on Muhammad's forehead. As he turns to draw his weapon, Muhammad is no more; his face is all over Sloane and the rear wall, "Fuck!" Snell helps him up, "What did he say? Anything important?" Sloane looks at the headless body on the floor; Snell shakes him, "Mike, what was his last words?" "Nothing. He just couldn't form the words. Whatever it was, the spirits on the other side will hear him." Snell gives his partner a curious stare as Sloane turns and leaves. "Ready to go home?" Sloane asks the girl, who nods and begins to walk with them, "T-Thank you sirs..." "Your welcome." Williams gets on the radio, "Base Command, this is Gofer Team. We have resolved the situation – entire team is functional, church leader is 187, and we also have victim and children in our care. Coming out now." "Roger Gofer Team, send in forensics?" "Roger Base Command, Team Gofer out." As they lead the children out of the church, a thought nags at Sloane, "Cassidy! Derek Cassidy's alive! Impossible...I killed him myself!" The sun finally comes out from behind the clouds to shine on the street below.

Book One: "I Declare War..."

It is useless to delude ourselves. All the restrictions, all the international agreements made during peacetime are fated to be swept away like dried leaves on the winds of war. A man who is fighting a life-and-death fight - as all wars are nowadays - has the right to use any means to keep his life. War means cannot be classified as human and inhuman. War will always be inhuman, and the means which are used in it cannot be classified as acceptable or not acceptable except according to their efficacy, potentiality, or harmfulness to the enemy.

The purpose of war is to harm the enemy as much as possible; and all means which contribute to this end will be employed, no matter what they are. He is a fool if not a patricide who would acquiesce in his country's defeat rather than go against those formal agreements which do not limit the right to kill and destroy, but simply the ways of killing and destroying. The limitations applied to the so called inhuman and atrocious means of war are nothing but international demagogic hypocrisies. As a matter of fact, poison gases are being experimented with everywhere - and certainly not for purely scientific purposes. Just because of its terrible efficacy, poison gas will be largely used in the war of the future. This is the brutal fact; and it is better to look it squarely in the face without false delicacy and sentimentalism.

General Giulio Douhet (1868 - 1930)

Chapter 1:

Five years later...

    The rounds sear past my face and hands like hot coals as my rounds ring out of my weapon like church bells in my ears. Anu, its been so long since I have fired a weapon, but it seems that I haven't lost my touch: two dead bodies in the corner and two more about to be. These guards are young and scared. My eyes are burning from the sweat as it comes down my face. Then suddenly, my gun stops - out of bullets. Quickly I duck behind the oak desk that I have been using as a shield and reload. Those young guards race forward cautiously yet ready to blast me away! "Come out fella! We got you dead to rights." "Y-Yeah! W-We got you cornered. Come out slow and easy." I look under the desk to see where they are and cock back my hammer, "Okay! I'm comin' just don't shoot, okay?" "A-Alright." The top of my head peeks out a little and then my eyes glance up to see them and then I duck back down. "Come out! NOW!" I quickly come up and lean to the left as my firing hand squeezes of two rounds toward them. As I fall to the ground, I see that each hits its mark: one in the chest, and one in the head. They both fall on top of each other and the last breath of life leaves their bodies.

I breathe hard, pick up the files and start to go through them. "Damn..." I notice a few of the faces. Some of these people I personally have met during my time as a Secret Service agent. Then I scan the clippings of reports and memos. The information is unbelievable! UFO intel, private meetings between Kennedy and Castro, correspondence between Hoover and Elijah Muhammad! Even faxes about the creation of a new biological agent - aimed at all of the 'miscreants and degenerates of American society that continue to be a festering leech on our way of life.' boy, Hoover and the Agency and his COINTELPRO people sure were long range... "FREEZE!!" I look up to see another guard running upon me simultaneously drawing his weapon and about to fire at me!

In one fluid motion, I drop the files and knock his weapon out of his hands and grab him, "You know what? I DON'T THINK SO!" as I hurl him across the room over the heavy oak desk. As I bend down once more, running feet approach my position. The door gets locked and I jump over the desk for cover. The knob is tried. The door is made into Swiss cheese and then they break it down, so I fire suppression rounds to discourage them. Suddenly, it gets quiet. Then I hear it, the setup of a LAWS rocket! "Shit. Time to go." I say to myself, while kicking out the window, which has seen a few bullets. As I put my handle to work, I hear the command: "FIRE!" The sound comes out like a wave crashing against the shore. It'll take less than a minute to cover the room and meet me, so I dive through into the air. The desk and bodies go as I feel the air hit my face.

It feels good. Clean and pure. I go down spread eagle so to slow my descent. Boy it feels so free up here! Until a bullet singes my ear! "Damn!!" I turn and start shooting back, upwards, which makes my descent go faster, but fuck it, y'know? The beating of propellers jump in my ears. I cast a quick look sideways and there they are: Coming after me. But I got go: I pull the cord and my chute explodes. My weapon does the same to the pilot. They hit their mark and the copper swerves for a bit, then crashes into the building and explodes. As I land and roll, gather my chute and toss it into the waiting car, and drive off, it finally comes to earth - crashing and exploding once again in front of the building.

The rain was coming down hard. Sounding like hail against my windowpane. A few hours earlier, my phone rang - I was in the middle of deep recollection when it did, "Hello?" "Snell, is that you?" "Yeah, who's this?" "Cassidy at the Bureau." Feds. I never liked them, too gung ho for my taste. "What you want with me, Cassidy?" I sip my drink. "Got a bird

on your wire. Faxing you the sheet now." The machine beeps. "Name?"
"Sloane, Michael Richard." I look at the picture.

Chapter 2:

"I know this guy." I tell myself. I sip my drink again. Yeah, I know
him - and his Company: Smoke. Bunch of Mercs to us grunts. Sloane was a
good man in the field; always came out on top in the firefights with the VC.
Damn good leader, damn good team too - so went the stories. Racked up
more legal kills than the Green Berets and Special Forces put together. I
was personally in a fight alongside Sloane and his men against some asshole
officers: didn't like officers of color. I smile and laugh at the memory, "Still
there Snell?" "Yeah, just reading." We beat those guys (and a few in the bar
as well) and his men almost beat them to death. And no one ever spoke of
the incident or bothered Sloane and his men ever again.

"What's he got to do with me? I'm just a homicide detective." "So
was he." I can hear the smoke leave his mouth as he blows it out. "When?"
"When his lady got whacked..." "WHAT?!? His wife?" Cassidy clears his
throat, "Yeah, right in front of him too. Y'see, they was shopping for
themselves and their baby in the oven when two asswipes came in and held
the place up and took her as a hostage." "Fuck" "As the asshole backed
toward the door, he pushes her away and blew her back out and the baby
out the front. Asshole got whacked of course." "Of course." "He ain't been
the same since." "Huh! I'll bet so." I down the rest of my drink, "So, what's
he got to do with me, Cassidy?" "Simple, he's on the run for murder, and he
lives in your town." I can feel him smiling. "Really? Why should I believe
you? My instincts and this paper tells me that he's your problem - not mine."
I punch up my info network and input the name. "Yes...he was ours a long
time ago. But after this...incident of murder, he's yours." "Who and where?"
"Records and Archives. He whacked five guards and destroyed an office and
made a helicopter crash, causing property damage." "He sounds like one of
those super solider types you boys created that got away, am I right?"
"That's classified." He replies coolly, "BULLSHIT!! If this was 'classified', you
wouldn't be talkin' to me - you Feds would have a total blackout on him and
his activities!" I slam down the phone and go back to my info. I page
back...start at the beginning.

The hole bursts with sound like a drop hitting a puddle. She falls to
her knees and I am frozen in my steps, unable to move. She calls my name
and reaches out to me with blood stained lips and her womb releasing our
child - who is soaked in blood and internal fluids, cries out in anger...anger
for being forced out too soon, too hard, too animalistic. She grabs our child
and scoops him up so that she doesn't crush him as she falls. Now I move,
my movements are all slow...so stiff that my arms feel like lead; my weapon
is an I-bar in my hands. The fiend, the animal who didn't give a shit about

my wife falls into pieces like a Road Runner cartoon, blood and bone everywhere. I now fall to my knees - holding my family - lost to me forever and I cry. I cry; clutching my stomach and pillow crying, "I'm sorry..." until my alarm clock rings.

I wake up covered in sweat and my eyes are all puffy and red from crying so much. I look around my bedroom: my stealth uniform and firearms are draped over the chair, the files I took are scattered all over the table. Pictures of us are all over the bed. I sit there and look them; why am I involved? Is it because this was my case? For Sonya and our baby? For a future which is now lost to me? Hopefully, when all this is finished, I will know. I gotta get outta here; fast. Cassidy and his Bureau hit squad are gonna be here...IF they haven't already. I jump to the window, which faces the street. All I see is a cable truck. I glance at the clock on the dresser and think: 'Maybe.' I take a quick hot shower and shave. Dress and check the street again and pack my gear. As I'm finishing loading my 9mm, my perimeter alarm sounds. "DAMN!!" I say to myself and I jet.

My front door turns into toothpicks as a crew of suits in riot gear come in my home and firing like crazy, hoping to hit me. Some come through the windows too, shooting my bed and making it like a Charles Manson victim. "CEASE FIRE! CEASE FIRE!!" calls the field leader. Quiet resumes. The footsteps crush glass, wood and plaster. I can see him in my mind: Derek Cassidy - fat ass been hounding me ever since Guam. "Where is he?" "No body chief." "SHIT! He's probably been gone--" "Negative. Our search team verified he was in the bedroom before we penetrated." The footsteps all head there. I'm beating feet the other way, toward the street. Lucky for me, I still kept this escape tunnel operational - under my house.

"Shit - you assholes do more damage than a John Woo flick." Cassidy says as he chews on his cigar; surveying the bedroom from the doorway: the window, which faces the street is shattered; the bed is shot to pieces; pictures are on the floor - shattered and full of holes. Cassidy walks and sits on the bed and sighs. Shaking his head in disbelief, he picks up a picture - surprisingly, it is Sloanes' wedding portrait. "Damn, pretty bitch." A smile glides on his face. His phone rings, "Cassidy." "Enjoying your handiwork?" surprise hits his face, "Sloane?" he gets up and in one fluid motion is at the window looking out, "Where the fuck are you?" His eyes dart across the street, "Wish you knew, pussy." "You got jokes, huh?" "Yup." "SIR!" "What?" Cassidy turns, "We've found an underground tunnel under the bed!!" "WHAT!?!" Sloane laughs in Cassidy's ear. Just then, simultaneously, the cable van explodes. The house rocks. Cassidy is thrown to the floor, "SHIT!!" Sloane laughs still; he exits the scene with a vehicle stashed around the corner. As he leaves, police sirens and fire engines are approaching towards him. He ducks and says before he leaves, "Hey Cassidy: That's for trespassing on my house." and Sloane speeds off.

Momentarily, at the scene of the chaos, with police cars cordon both sides of the street, policemen keeping neighbors back and stopping reporters, Homicide Detective Maximillian Snell walks in the house, pissed to hell, "Cassidy! What the hell are you doing? Is THIS how you suits handle one of yours?" Back up cop. This is government business, you have no jurisdiction -" "Oh yes I do. *You* called me on this remember?" "*Only as a formality*. I didn't have to notify you; as you told me: I could have a total blackout on this." "But you didn't, *this* is a crime scene - it's my jurisdiction." "Not even." Cassidy edges toward Snell, chewing on his cigar, "Back the fuck up! You beat walking bitch, before I --" Snell grabs Cassidy and pulls him forward, driving his knee deep into his stomach; making Special Agent Cassidy lose all of his air.

As Cassidy lies on the decimated floor gasping for air, Snell squats down and leans in toward his ear, "Now, don't fuck with *me*." He gets up and turns to leave, "Let's give these suits room to do their job and then we'll do ours." As he leaves the house, his commanding officer drives up, angry and surprised, "Snell!! What the hell is this?" he demands with a wave of his arm and pointing, "Calm down chief, wasn't me - Feds." "Feds? You mean about that phone conversation earlier this morning?" "Yep." Snell sits on the chief's car, "My instincts and that fax I got tells me that Cassidy wants this Sloane guy bad; really bad. Inside, it looks like a 'shoot first - fuck the questions' kind of scenario." He lights a cigarette, "You sure Max?" Snell exhales, "Not all the way, just hunches and gut feelings plus..." "What?" Snell waves it away, "Give me time and I'll have proof." "Give it to me - and no dead bodies, understand?" Snell smiles a little, "I'll try." He flicks away the cigarette as Cassidy and his team leave the bullet riddled home of Michael R. Sloane:

Hunted Man.

Chapter 3:

Cassidy radios in to his helicopter, "Anything Eagle Two? Over."
"Roger Nest, spotted a vehicle leaving the scene in a big hurry." "What is
it?" he asks excitedly, "It's a gray convertible, all beat up." "Location?" "On
the highway - heading north on I 28." "Intercept and detain by any means,
I'm enroute." "Roger." He motions his arms to signal the order, "Let's
move! Get mobile - pronto!" and they all get into vehicles and speed off.
Seeing this, Snell gets into his own car and follows, "SHIT! The hound has a
scent." Meanwhile, Eagle Two zeroes in on the speeding convertible. The
pilot radios to the sniper who is waiting patiently, "Will have him in range in
T-minus 20 seconds." "Roger, lining up my sights now." Sloane, taking in
the traffic, just now notices the sound of the beating helicopter blades as it
nears him. "Hmnh?" He adjusts his rearview mirror and spots them.

"Damn!" he hits the accelerator and zigs through the traffic, trying to
make himself a hard-to-hit target. Irregardless, the pilot begins to fire
rounds from the turret - all random shots. Hitting concrete and tires of other
cars and foliage as its intended target swerves and dodges cars, trucks,
explosions and debris to avoid being hit. "Keep it at this level." the sniper
commands the pilot, he has a clear shot of Sloane in the scope and fires.
Luckily the rounds hit the trunk and back seat. Reactively, Sloane ducks,
"Shit!" He looks back quickly and continues his evasive maneuvering. As he
looks in the passenger side mirror, he notices that he is way ahead of the
traffic, but the gunship is still on his tail and gaining ground, He slams the
brake pedal and screeches to a halt. Quickly, he sits on the front seat and
aims his pistol at the oncoming helicopter, when his sights are aligned, he
fires in rapid succession as it passes over him. "Damn!!" the pilot says as
he sways to and fro.

Sloane takes the car off the freeway and through the bushes, hoping
to lose his pursuers in the dense foliage. As the branches hit him and the
windshield, he still hears the beating of the propellers and the firing of the
gun turret. He takes the vehicle to the bright light at the end of the foliage,
which is a cliff; so Sloane bails out rolling with the fall and reaching for the
duffel bag, pulling out a LAWS rocket launcher and waits. The vehicle has
crashed and exploded on the lower freeway upon impact. Slowing down his
breathing, and waiting patiently, the intended target appears right over the
wreckage. "Eagle Two to Nest, target's vehicle is crashed and burned. No
visual as yet of body; still searching."

As the pilot radios in to Cassidy, the sniper spots Sloane on the cliff
and just as he turns his weapon to fire, Sloane releases the LAWS rocket.
The sniper quickly barks out: "PULL UP!! PULL UP PRONTO!!" But the pilot
hears him too late.

With the trajectory and angle of the path, the rocket hits the helicopter directly inside the passenger area, exploding and turning the inside to nothing. The sniper goes flying out the other end from the impact and lands in the middle of the traffic below; getting run over by a 18-wheeler cargo truck. The helicopter falls and crashes on the cliff side and rolls down toward the traffic, still aflame. Cassidy, with a look of complete and utter disbelief, simply hangs up, "Fucking shit. I knew we should have killed him back in Guam." He looks out the window as his second-in-command asks, "What now, sir?" "Send damage control over to the wreckage site and report in with what they find. Driver! Back to headquarters." The driver responds, "Yes sir." and raises the tinted window. Meanwhile, a few cars back Max Snell wonders and turns off at the next exit, "Guam huh? Gotta make a phone call and schedule a meeting." He smiles as ideas fly through his head; Sloane continues with his getaway on foot. As he nears the highway, He thinks to himself, "Funny how easy it all comes back..."

Police Department: Homicide Squad.

"I need that file! Pronto!! (Sigh) Look, I don't care if it is classified - you owe me! Yeah, tomorrow...thanks." He hangs up the phone, gathers the files and notes he has in his possession, rises and proceeds toward the Chief of Detectives, Homicide Division's office. A knock hits the wired pane and the voice bids entry. "Sit down Snell." "Thanks." Detective Snell plops down into the couch, lights up a cigarette and exhales, "What you got so far?" the Chief asks, "Well, so far I got all of Mike Sloane's story when he joined the force." he flips open a few pages of notes to the desired entry, "*This guy was something*: he bought down that Mafia hit guy - Raze, and was the head of the investigation of that cult, The Newborn Legion and its leader Prince Allah Abdul Muhammad; when his wife and child was murdered in that botched store robbery. He's been on stress leave ever since." The Chief turns in his chair and taps his pen upon his chin, a question forms in his mind as he goes over what information Snell just dropped, "What about before he became a cop?" "I got my main contact sending me that information tomorrow." The smoke exits his mouth. The Chief looks out the window, "Good. What's your opinion on the ruckus this morning?"

Snell sighs and puffs on his cigarette, "Well, judging by the house, its like I said before, this Fed wants him six feet deep - badly. Once I get the info from my contact, I'll be able to make a plan and strategy. But, for now I got the Feds tailed." "Be careful, I don't want this whole department accused of harassment or impeding an investigation, understand?" "Always." Snell puts out the cigarette and leaves. Halfway to his desk, the Chief calls him back, "Yeah?" "I almost forgot to tell you - you got a new partner on this." a look of disgust crosses his face, "Hell no! Chief, you know me. I work best alone..." "I know, but I don't want any high flying 'Lethal Weapon' shit out of you. I want backup to cover your ass. This shit is sounding too big." Snell sighs and shakes his head, "Okay Chief, when?" "Tomorrow, same time as your information arrives." "Thanks for nothing." Snell slams the door, "Don't mention it." and Lt. Williams smiles.

In the meantime, Sloane has changed his clothes and found a payphone. He looks around him and sighs a breath to calm himself. He closes his eyes to remember the phone number and prays that he is still there. After putting in the proper toll, he dials. The phone rings at least six times before a voice answers, "What's the word?" Sloane replies slowly, "The black razor has blood on it." The sound of the receiver dropping and hitting the floor rings in his ear. "Damn! Holy shit! I-Its you. Can you come in?" His eyes dart around the streets, "Yeah, I'm on foot so give me some time. You still at the same locale?" "Roger, See you soon." "Out." The connection is ended. He exits the phone booth and continues to his destination.

"DAMMIT! Fucking son of a bitch!" Cassidy roars at the pictures and files scattered on the table. "You fucking bastard!" He screams at the pictures he has in his hand, "You should've died in Guam with your buddies..." He screams as he relives the memory:

Chapter 4:

The Mission: Prevent an Asian power bloc to form an united front to control the world market in goods and services.

The Team: The Black Razors - Team Leader, Michael Richard Sloane; Second in Command, J. Jackson; Demolitions, Xavier Roberts; Infiltration, Charles Downing and Information Acquisition, Jericho Loche; with Observation and Intelligence, Central Intelligence Agency and Federal Bureau of Investigations Liaison Derek Cassidy.

The room is quiet. Smoke wafts around the heads like an ominous spectre. Cassidy looks at the men gathered who comprise this team, chewing on his Cuban cigar. "All hand picked by me." he thinks to himself. He inhales and exhales viciously, "Its simple gentlemen: WE go in and prevent this summit meeting from taking place." "When is it?" Sloane asks. "In one week. It's *supposed* to be a secret meeting, but as you know, WE know all about it." He smiles as he pulls up a map of the country, "We go in tonight and take out the main principal speakers in the summit. Anyone we miss, we get them at the shindig. Any questions?" Sloane looks at his men, no one answers. "Good. Here's the main target: General Sum Dray Ngoy, officer in the Chinese army with powerful political connections throughout the Asian network. It was his idea to unify the Asian countries since Guam is about to be self supporting soon and monopolize the foreign economic business structure, since a majority of American products are made in these countries; greedy bastards! Eating the whole pie and leaving us with the crumbs off the pan. " A picture goes up on the screen, "Assignments are still the same - I'll be baby-sitting while you professionals handle the wetwork. Remember, we have to be quick, in and out like ghosts. For as soon we hit the General, the whole summit would be covered like a blanket. Loche, gather intel like there ain't no tomorrow, because if you fail, tomorrow will be under a red Asian sun. Just take it easy on the hallucinogenics and truth serum, alright?" Loche snorts and grins, "Whatever, man." Cassidy passes out files to each man, "Here are your intel and targets. We meet again at 0200 hours and be in the air by 0300. Be ready." Cassidy walks out, a trail of smoke wafting behind him.

End of Book One.

Book Two: "Proportion"

Terrorism. The word, of course, has a pejorative connotation. We have freedom fighters; groups to whom we are indifferent have guerrillas. Our enemies employ terrorists. Terrorism is a species of evasive war and counter evasive war; it is quite simply a discriminate war of evasion and counter evasion. It is correct to say that war is politics by other means. The common use of the word 'terrorism' appears to classify terrorism as political and particular warlike, rather than as merely criminal in particularly violent criminals. The main objection to the view that terrorism be equated with indiscriminate land warfare of evasion derives from the natural belief that terrorism has something to do with terror. It is for example, is not terrorism to be equated with military operations aimed to induce terror or to be effective via terror? There is a very widespread tendency to connect the word terrorism, not with the bombing by one state of the cities, towns, villages of another but with that cluster of contemporary phenomenon which includes: guerrilla war, counter insurgency, wars of national liberation, struggles against colonialism, peasant wars, etc.

Our definition is that a person's activity may be acquiesce of indiscriminate warfare of evasion regardless of his attitude to the inducement of terror as opposed to victims. Assassination campaign in which no effort is made at discrimination or in which the killing is deliberately indiscriminate is a campaign of terrorism. A campaign of indiscriminate killing as part of the warfare of counter evasion is terrorism. To continue, a terrorist is the fiercer or glamorous stranger of whose activity our theoretical understanding is very poor and very thin. One is apt to think of the terrorist as however sympathetic, a ruthless figure prepared to use indiscriminate violence in pursuit of a well-defined goal. To wage war because one thinks one has no alternative or because one believes that war is the only way to show that one is is in earnest is not necessarily to do something which one assumes is understandable, but justifiable as some means to an end.

War, as defined by Quincy Wright, "...a violent contact of distinct but similar entities. And in this sense of the word, a collision of stars; a fight between a lion and a tiger, a battle between two primitive tribes, and hostilities between two modern nations would all be war...the legal condition which equally permits two or more hostile groups to carry on a conflict by armed force." The military dimension; if and only it can be understood, explained, justified, etc., or by reference to fighting which has these four characteristics:
    A. It is always likely to be fighting to the death; i.e. to the death of individual human beings.
    B. The fighting, very likely to the death that we have in mind is fighting between groups, organised for such fighting or between such

organized groups and disorganized or unorganized opponents.
    C. The fighting we have in mind employs weapons designed for the purpose.
    D. The fighting we have in mind is inseperatable from quarrels over matters relating to whatever the fundamental categories are in which the people living in that world understand their social, political, religious or economic, etc. life.

    The aggressor/defender theory of war; it is possible in real situations to distinguish between aggressors and defenders and the kind of conduct which is permitted to the defender in quite different from that to be expected of the aggressor.

    Proportion; the striking of a balance between means and ends such that the overall outcome of the chosen course of war is better than all available alternatives.

The Ethics of War by Barrie Paskins & Michael Dockrill
Pages: 86, 89, 90, 91-94, 102, 105, 106, 191, & 211

Chapter 1:

    0400 hours. We are now over the Pacific Ocean, getting ready to cross the International Date Line. The bird is a gunship and Medivac all in one. My eyes dart across at my team: J. Jackson, my second in command. Xavier Roberts, Demolitions expert. If he don't have it, he'll build it, a regular MacGuyver; Charlie Downing, my fellow ninja. He can creep in, and do the job more quieter than a church mouse. And snoring his head off in the corner, is my 'Information Gatherer', Jericho Loche; swears he's the baddest motherfucker on the planet until that tussle we had this morning on the flightline.

    "What the hell are you doing?" "What it look like? I'm getting my mind ready for the trip." He puffs some more on the joint. Angrily. I smack it out of his mouth, "Yo! What the fuck!?! That shit cost me 40 balls!" "That shit is gonna get you killed." "You owe me 40 balls, Sloane." "I don't owe you shit." I turn to walk away. As my second step hits the pavement, he's upon me. Grabbing my head and pulling it back, he's trying to kill me! I quickly thrust two elbows into his ribs and flip him over my shoulder and land my fist dead into his nose, hearing the crack as my knuckles drive through the bone and cartilage. "Aargh!" I pick him up and elbow him in the jaw for good measure. He almost breaks his skull on the tarmac but Downing catches him. "Dammit Mike! You almost killed him!" "He almost killed me." I walk to the transport and climb aboard to inspect it. I feel a hand upon my shoulder. "Proved your point?" "Yep." J. always was the coolest of us two.

"Sometimes I don't know whose crazier, you or Jericho." "Probably me, I don't smoke." I smile and he laughs. As we finish up our inspection and checks, the smell of a cigar invades my nostrils, "Sloane!" "What Cassidy?" "What happened to Loche? His face looks like hamburger." "I happened to it. Are you ready for this?"

He climbs in, wearing green fatigues and a 9mm handgun, followed by a case which looks like it can hold a body with no problem, "You bet!" And he smiles. Sloane looks at the bag and nods towards it. Jackson shakes his head and sits next to Cassidy, "What's in the bag? Your lunch?" "Fuck you Jackson, its "insurance"." and he blows a puff of smoke at him. "Insurance?" Sloane asks, "Insurance for whom?" "You never mind with the inquisition Sloane, you got your orders - follow them and I'll follow mine, capice?" "Yassur, boss, sir." and Jackson laughs. "Alright, time to go." Jackson gives the signal and they jump in. Loche gives Sloane a killing look as he enters the transport. Sloane gives him the finger.

Real Time: "Chocolate City" the black neighborhoods of Washington DC A ghetto where survival of the fittest rings everyday. Sloane comes to a street corner and looks down both ends of the street. A Toyota Land Cruiser goes by him, playing its music very loud. Its occupants eye him with distrust and wonder, he looks at them with distaste, "Think they're the baddest niggas on the planet. Non-submitting fools." And he walks across the street toward a battered townhouse. He looks at it and takes a deep breath. Gripping the handrail, he climbs the stairs and rings the bell, then he knocks on the door. After ten seconds, He bangs on the door again. An angry voice screams through it, "Shit motherfucker!! Wait a damned minute!" Sloane hears squeaks and squeals from behind the door. Instinctively, he reaches for his weapon, a modified Tech -9 assault weapon. "Who the hell is it?" the voice calls from behind the door, "If you's Jehovah's Witnesses, I don't want to be bothered!!"

Sloane laughs at the comment, "The razor's got blood on it." The voice behind the door goes silent. "Shit." it says quietly. Locks and bolts are pulled open and turned. The door swings open slowly. Sloane takes a step back and squints his eyes to see in the dim foyer. When his eyes adjust, he can't believe his eyes, "Shit." When the wheel stops in the doorway, Sloane now sees his former information contact as a paraplegic. "What's up, G? You looking mighty worse for wear, dog. Come inside and rest." "Thanks, sure." Alfonso Christophe Tracy, formerly standing at six feet and one inches tall, military veteran who served in both versions of Desert Storm, now permanently confined to a wheelchair since his body has been diagnosed with, "Cancer, Mike...the big 'C'. Got that shit fucking around with ol' Sadaam..." "But Fonzo, how did you get put in a wheelchair?" Sloane asks as he sits down. Fonzo spins back around, facing him, "This? You don't remember?" Sloane shakes his head no, "This happened after that Guam trip you guys took with Cassidy!" Sloane's eyes goes wide then down to slits as his anger begins to boil, "Cassidy? Derek Cassidy did this to you?" "Yep, basically, his boys did all the work; he just gave the order. Told you they had you tagged. Want anything to drink?" He spins around again and heads for the kitchen. "Yeah, a cold brewski if you got one." Sloane looks at his old friends' domicile. Surprised that its so laid out in a relaxed style since the outside looks so shitty, "In your face camouflage." He notices some pictures on the shelf, "I'll be damned..." he thinks to himself. In the pictures are Fonzo, Sonya and him; at Sonya's college graduation. Other pictures are of Fonzo with some women and at a black tie function. "Yeah, biggest night of my life." He says as he pulls up next to Sloane and hands him his beer, "I was getting an award from the Dead Poets Society and I had invited the Last Poets and Griot Foday Musa Suso to attend with me. Boy was those Caucasians shocked when we stepped into the joint!" Fonzo laughs big and hearty, tears fall down the sides of his face. "Yeah, a really big night, we turned the place out. Showed them how its supposed to be done."

Guam Time: "Now, you professionals show these gooks how its supposed to be done, got it?" "We got it Cassidy, you do your job, and we'll do ours." Sloane says coldly. Cassidy looks at him venomously, "Alright, get ready!" The transport comes in low, under the radar of the military base, which occupies the island of Guam. Sloane runs a quick background check on the island in his mind: 'located in the western central part of the Pacific Ocean, Guam is an United States territory. Its chief importance to the US is as a military base midway between America and Asia. It was first discovered by Ferdinand de Magellan in 1521, Spain claimed it from the 16th Century A.C.E. till the end of the 19th Century. After Spain lost the Spanish-American war in 1898, Guam became US possession. The Guamanian people are US citizens, but they can't vote in national US elections - reminds me of the Jim Crow laws for Africans after slavery ended.' The unit hit the ground and runs toward the dense foliage, each man hitting the ground to provide cover for the next man if snipers or others are aware of their arrival. Sloane gives the silent sign for moving and they are off. Cassidy lands at the Military installation, puffing on his cigar as an officer greets him, "Sir! We weren't aware of your coming." He waves the man away, "It's alright, base commander knows I'm here on Agency business, don't concern yourselves with me. I'll be in my quarters in officer's housing - I don't want to be disturbed, understand?" "Yes sir!" and Cassidy walks and enters the staff car and leaves the flight line, smiling.

Chapter 2:

Washington DC: Metropolitan Police Department Detective Division, Homicide Squad.

Max Snell is going over the previous days report, ballistics, and coroner's data when a light tap hits his desk. He doesn't look up, "Yeah?" "I'm looking for a Lt. Williams." the voice responds. "Straight ahead, first door with his name on it." Snell points from behind the files. "Thanks." the voice says and walks away. "Dames..." Snell thinks to himself, as he notices a description of the bodies at the Federal Building: all but one was shot before the missile took out the whole office. The two guards who were killed next to each other were shot at close range, but with only one bullet apiece before either one got a return shot off! "Fucking marksman you are Sloane." "Snell!" His superior calls out. "Yeah?" "Get in here." Snell grumbles and folds up the files and sticks them in his drawer and proceeds toward the office. He knocks and is granted entry. His superior, LT. Williams is a statuesque person, topping off at almost 7 feet; expert field tactician; husky build with grey around the temples and a receding afro. Today he is wearing a white shirt with an open collar covered by an open sleeveless vest.

"What's up chief?" He asks, rubbing his eyes. The Lt. smiles and motions, "Meet your new partner, Detective Teresa Franklin." Snell looks at her with a look of complete surprise and takes stock of her. He is speechless, "What's wrong Detective? Never had a woman for a partner before?" The LT. smirks and replies, "Not really; since the last female detective partner he had quit before they left the building." "Really?" "Must have been his 'charming personality' " She smirks, "I can imagine." "Oh, hell no chief! Are you nuts? Put her on with someone else!" "No buts Snell, she's it and that is that. Goodbye, don't get shot on your first day Detective Franklin." "I'll be careful LT. Thank you." They leave the Lt.'s office, with Snell huffing and puffing and lighting up a cigarette and glancing back at his new partner, "Goddamn woman, they gives me a goddamn woman! Jesus H. fucking Christ!" He slams into his chair and pulls out the file again, mumbling. Franklin looks around for a seat or a desk but doesn't see one, "Where is my desk?" "Get one." "Can I use yours in the meantime?" He looks at her, pondering, "Okay." She lays her purse on the desk, Snell puts his feet right on top of it. Smoke rises from behind the files. She looks at his feet and then at the files that he is holding, "Men: gotta show their ass." She whistles a little bit, grabs his feet and flips him up and out of his chair; the files go scattered all over the floor and covering Snell, who has a look of complete astonishment on his face. As he looks up at Detective First Grade. Franklin, who is wearing a Chino blazer with a matching pants and white open collar shirt , stands looking down at him with a wide grin on her face -

and the other officers are behind her all agape. "What the hell Franklin?!?" "At least you remembered my name." She sits in his chair and begins to pick up and gather together the scattered files as Snell rises off the floor, dusting himself. "Dames..." He says as he walks to the men's room.

Guam Time: The Black Razors: a team of five men, each a specialist in their field. The sun is beginning to rise as they approach the middle of Mount Alitan. Even before dawn, the heat is unbearable. A minor cool breeze floats in from the Philippine Sea, but it isn't enough. Loche takes a drink from his canteen, Sloane cuts away at branches while Downing and Roberts scout ahead for booby traps and Jackson guards the rear. Jackson swings the mighty M-80 machine gun and listens. Birds and insects chatter away simultaneously with Sloane's cutting. As he begins to turn to join the others, a signal from Roberts stops the others and they hit the ground, letting the dense foliage hide them.

Real Time: The Federal Building, which is the main office of Derek Cassidy's Special Operations Organization; situated on the top three floors overlooking the city. Cassidy is in his office, looking out the window, a Cuban cigar nestled firmly between his teeth, lit and smoking, "Where are you Sloane? You've couldn't have gone far on foot..." The phone rings. He turns and pushes a button, "What." "Sir, he used a LAWS rocket on our bird--" "So?" "So, he was expecting us sir. Do you think he knows?" "Not likely Mr. Steinbaker. Not likely. Get the GPS system on his tail and relay me any findings, clear?" "Yes sir." The line disconnects. He looks down at the photos and stacks of intelligence on his enemy. He then begins to pin each photo up on a bulletin board in order of possible loopholes, allies or wild cards. He stands back and looks at the picture of Michael Sloane. His hand runs across the table and he throws a pushpin at the photo; it hits in the middle of the forehead, "Bang, bitch!" and he laughs.

"So, what's up with you now, G?" Fonzo asks. Sloane slumps in the couch and takes a deep breath. He runs his hands through his hair and over his beard, gathering his thoughts. He looks at Fonzo, "Okay, I'm on the run..." "No shit Sherlock." "Cassidy is after me..." "Again? When are you just gonna kill that sonofabitch, huh? Damn Mike! Just kill him and we'll all live happily ever after like a fucking fairy tale!!" "Isn't that simple anymore. He now runs a covert Agency." "Oh, you mean the Special Operations Organization? I been knew about that." Sloane looks at his friend in utter disbelief, "Y-You knew...?" "Yeah! C'mon, I'll show you." Fonzo turns and begins to rotate his wheels toward what looks like a closet. His hand touches a panel and the door moves and opens. Sounds of machinery and voices envelope Sloanes' ears. When they enter, he sees multiple television screens covering a whole wall and computer screens covering another; at least three terminals are running. All over the floor are faxes and printouts from somewhere. "Damn G. This all yours?" "Yep, I own the whole brownstone so I had a few friends come in and do all this for me." Sloane edges over to some printouts on the floor to his right, "May I?" "Sure." He picks them up and looks at them. Then he flips a page and quickly scans it; and then another. He looks at Fonzo, who is sipping on a glass of Sprite, "T-This is all about Cassidys' whole operation!" "Yep. You're all over the news G..." Sloane glances up at the television screens, He spies one that has his house in the background, "Shit." "Let me see what you got, then go lay down on that table over there." "Why?" "To check you out for implants." Fonzo says plainly.

"Okay." and Sloane hands him the files that he retrieved from the Federal Building. Then he makes his way over to the table and gets on it, "Strip Mike." Fonzo says without looking up from the files. Sloane complies.

Guam Time: Voices are heard coming through the brush. Laughter and the smell of liquor precedes them. Loche readies his blade from its sheath on his right boot. When the voices come closer, Sloane notices that it is just some local farmers and he quickly gives the signal to stop and resume their previous stance. Loche lets out a low "Fuck." under his breath and spits off to the side. Sloane gives the call for all clear to Roberts and Downing and they give another call for their presence immediately at their position, which is at the end of the trail of the mountain. When the others arrive, Downing points toward what is below them, "There it is Chief: Santa Rita, the meeting place. What's next?" "Good job, Charlie. Now we go down and make camp at the base of this mountain and recon the area." Loche grumbles, "Why can't we just hit it now? They's asleep!" Sloanes' face is a look of irritation, "Because Jeri, we're tired and we don't know the lay of the land. Alot's changed since last we were here. Now, let's go." And they proceed down the mountain.

Chapter 3:

Real Time: The medical ultrasound scanner proceeds over Sloane's torso. He lifts his head nervously as it goes past his groin area. "Don't worry, it won't harm you." Fonzo says with a chuckle as his eyes monitor the readout on the screen. He taps the headset mike, "Stop." "What?" Sloane asks. Fonzo is silent as he turns toward the examination table. His hand presses buttons on his wheelchair, "Marcia, please come assist." "On the way." the English accented voice replies. "W-Who is Marcia?" Fonzo stops at the spot where the ultrasound is hovering over, "She's a former British Intelligence agent with a medical background and she's my care provider."

The doors slide open and the room floods with light. "Who needs to be stitched up, love?" Marcia says as she comes closer to the table. "Take a look." She quickly scans the monitor and looks back at Sloane. "Is it bad?"

"No. It's just a small tracer on your pelvic bone...actually, its *inside* your pelvic bone. That's gonna take some time to remove with the laser, love." Fonzo looks at Sloane and rubs his hands over his face, "This is something out of my league god. That's why Marcia's gonna do the operation." "A tracer?!?" "Yeah, seems its been there since Guam...Cassidy's been tracking you for a long time. But we're gonna cut off his pager system so keep still, okay?" Sloane shakes his head as Marcia preps for the procedure.

Guam Time: As the team reaches the mountain base, its dusk. Insects and birds chirp all around them. Sloane is sitting on a boulder and surveying Santa Rita with a telescope while the other are making the necessary quarters and preparations for the early morning raid. "Xavier!" "Yeah?" "Front and center." Xavier double times it to Sloane. "Sir." Sloane gives him a pencil and paper, "I need you to recon the area and make a quick sketch of the compound, any opposition and escape routes, 10-4?" "Roger." and he goes off into the underbrush. Sloane walks back to the small camp to insure everything is ready. He looks at the tunnels, tripwires made to warn of intruders. Once they meet with his approval, he goes to Jackson's tent. "J. it's me." "C'mon in." When he enters, he sees the map of the country laid out on Jackson's 'bed'. "Any ideas?"

Real Time: "Not a one." Snell slams the file shut and mumbles. Reaching in his desk drawer, pulling out a cigarette and lights it. "That stuff will kill you." Franklin says, "Its either this or some punk with a Tech-9." She smiles and nods. Snell looks over the photos of the crime scene at Sloane's home. "Come on." He gets up and she follows, "Where to?" "Sloane's house. I wanna check it over myself."

"This will take a few minutes, Mr. Sloane. So please keep still, okay love?" "S-Sure." Fonzo monitors the screen as Marcia prepares to use the surgical laser and x-ray surgeon's glasses. "A little to the left girl...there!" "Be very still. You will feel a little burning sensation - don't move." A low hum is heard in the still quiet room and it begins to penetrate his skin. Sloane clenches his teeth at the pain and balls his hands into fists, "Shit!" "She's almost done Mike." Fonzo reassures. "Sir! We got a lock on Sloane's whereabouts." "About damn time Mr. Steinbaker. Where is he?" Cassidy demands as the cigar smoke wafts around the room. "Will have lock in about 2 minutes." "Good." "Dammit! GPS got a fix on us! How much left?" "Almost...done!" Marcia goes, wiping her brow. "Dammit!! Sir, we lost it." Cassidy is silent. He taps the ashes into the ashtray and puffs on the cigar again. His eye spies the picture of Fonzo on the table, and he puts his cigar out on it. "Find me Alphonse Tracy - NOW!!" "Y-Yes sir!"

Fonzo quickly positions himself in front of a computer terminal and begins to type. His hands move so fast that it sounds like ants marching across a table. As Marcia puts coconut oil over the spot of Sloane's pelvis, he asks, "What are you doing?" "Creating a virus so they can't track us anymore. Back in the day, I always used other routes to access the GPS system, but they got a little smarter this time, but not smart enough!" and his finger presses the ENTER key. A coughing sound is heard through the speakers and the screen goes blank. Then it boots up again.

Guam Time: Cassidy's notebook boots up and he immediately punches keys to access his database link. A satellite rotates and positions itself over the Pacific Ocean. When the screen that he wants appears, he puts on his headset and radios Sloane and his team, "Black Razor this is Black Eagle. Are you situated? Over." Silence is heard for a moment then Sloane's voice comes over, "Black Eagle, I thought this was a radio silence mission, over?" "Don't worry about that, Black Razor. Is the penetration scheduled?" "Roger. Penetration is primed, ready and on schedule. Go to sleep Black Eagle." and Sloane cuts off transmission. Cassidy smirks and puffs on the cigar as he looks out into the clear night sky.

Real Time: The sky is clear and the moon is full. Her eyes stare at the stars that form around it. She begins to name constellations, "What the hell are you doing?" Snell gruffly asks as the car cuts around a corner, doing 60 mph. "Just remembering my lessons." she goes as a small smile creeps on her mouth. "We're here." the wheels squeal and grate across the curb. Doors slam. Footsteps peck across the sidewalk and up the cobblestone steps to be greeted by yellow police tape. Snell looks around the area and cast his eyes at Franklin; she nods and he breaks the tape. The knob is turned and they enter the foyer, "Goddamn..." Detective Franklin says as she surveys the mess left by Cassidy and his hit team.

Snell turns on a flashlight and shines it on the walls. Franklin shines hers on the floor and over the debris, "Damn! You weren't kidding. They wanted to smoke his ass." "Yep, they stormed in here shooting first. No recon, no word of warning..."

"No warning whatsoever! The government had this planned as a countermeasure if their 'New World Order' didn't pan out. Fuckin' bastards!!" Fonzo spews out from behind clenched teeth. Marcia brings him a glass and gives Sloane an ice pack for his pelvic region. "Yeah, that's what I found too. It started when we did that raid on a Brotherhood of the Dragon/Newborn Legion cult back when I was a cop." He motions for a pillow and Marcia places it on the soft side, "It was in there that Prince Allah Abdul Muhammad told me himself about the secret plot." "He knew?!?" "Yep. He was the co-funder in the project and was starting to name names when one of his own guys shot him. I of course, filled him full of bullets." Silence fills the room. Fonzo just stares into space. A vein twitches and pulses as he puts together the facts, rumors and documents that he has seen for years and pulls out a list of guilty organizations: "The FDA, WHO, the CDC, AMA and quite possibly some of the larger drug companies like Glaxco-Wellcom are in this with Congress, the FBI, CIA as well as Cassidy's SO Organization." He pulls up to Sloane, "Cassidy's probably the top man facilitating this "test run" in these cities, Mike; he's could also be the brain behind all this!" He rolls over to a controlling terminal and brings up the country with certain areas highlighted.

"This is where he escaped from them." Snell says as he raises the bullet-riddled bed and shows her the escape tunnel. "Its been preserved and kept operational for a long time. Our boy knew he was gonna get hit." "Are you saying that Sloane knew Cassidy was gunning for him? T-That this is some long-standing feud between two government agents? What does Sloane know or have that this Cassidy would kill and destroy everything Sloane has to get it?" Snell looks around the bedroom, "Dunno, but I'm betting it's something big." His light falls on a broken picture frame. Franklin picks it up, "This must've been his wife..." Her face grimaces, her eyes squint, "What's the matter?" "I-I don't know, but I feel like I should know her."

"These are the areas outlined in the report: Los Angeles, California; a militia in Michigan; Atlanta, Georgia; and finally here in Washington DC's black district." His voice drops at the thought of the gas infiltrating the community and he bangs his fist on the table, "Dammit! That fucking sonofabitch!" He looks at Sloane, "We've got to stop him Mike!" tears roll down Fonzo's face, "*WE* have to stop him, okay? Just like old times: me and you against the world. Another funk nappy mission. Are you down?" Michael Sloane stands up and walks over to his old friend, puts out his hand and they shake and hug, he looks dead into Fonzo's eyes, "Down for whatever. Down with you, Fonz." and they smile.

Washington DC: In the kitchen area of the White House, Secret Service Agent J. Jackson is eating his lunch and reading the newspaper. Overhead, the television is on, with a late news story. "Earlier today we reported to you about the raid on former DC Homicide Investigations Detective Michael Richard Sloane's home by Federal Agents. Although Det. Sloane was not home when they arrived, local police Detective Snell and a Federal Agent in-charge were reported to have gotten into a heated argument over jurisdiction and procedure..." He looks up when Sloane's name is mentioned and turns up the TV volume, "...a wreckage of a military gunship was found out on the freeway where it was reported by eyewitnesses that the gunship was firing rounds and pursuing an automobile which was returning fire as it sped through the traffic. Others report that the car was last seen crashing at an adjoining freeway, soon followed by the gunship's own wreckage. Experts claimed that a LAWS rocket fired from the adjoining cliff brought it down. Casualties have not been released..."

Jackson turns off the television. His face is one of fury, rage and pain.

His hands squeeze the ends of the table and his mind races back to their last mission in Guam...

Guam Time: Dusk. The cool breeze relaxes the team while Sloane and Jackson go over their attack formation and targets, "I'm going after the main speaker, the general himself. You got the secretary of the Foreign Relations Committee, Xavier and Charley got the main group of bodyguards and Loche has the pleasure of getting info out of whomever before we come in and wreck shop." Jackson laughs, "Sounds like a plan to me. What's the backup?" "Simple" Sloane replies, "Kill everyone and blow up the building if it goes bad."

End of Book Two.

Book Three: "The Tactics of Guerrilla Warfare"

"War is always a struggle in which each contender tries to annihilate the other."

- Ernesto 'Che' Guevara

Strategy (guerrilla terms): *The analysis of the objectives to be achieved in the light of the total military situation and the overall ways of reaching these objectives. i.e.. means in men, in mobility, in popular support, in armaments, in capacity of leadership on which he can count.*

- Have good knowledge of surrounding countryside.

Sloane's home. Snell and Franklin survey the damage caused by Cassidy and his federal hit squad. Franklin picks up a picture of Sloane and his wife, she looks at it for a few moments; her eyes squint and blink as a haze of fog lifts from her brain. Memories of laughter enter her ears; visions of two girls playing in a grassy field, hoola hoops and various assorted toys litter the ground around them. The sun shines high in the clear blue sky as a voice calls to them. They look and see a tall figure waving his arm, "Lunch time!" he goes. When he turns to return to the house, a bullet pierces his chest and another penetrates his brain. The tall man vaults backwards to the cool grass below him and dies. The two girls scream and run toward the man. Their eyes soaked with streaming tears when a grinning Asian points a long sword at them. He draws it back and runs it through the little girl.

"Hey! Are you okay?" Snell jolts her from her reverie. He looks at her face, sweat beads cover her forehead. A look of agitation emit from her eyes. Snell notices the hand which is holding the picture is shaking. She looks at Snell and then back at the picture. "Are you okay?" He asks again, more cautious and concerned as he looks directly into her eyes. "Y-Yeah. Yeah, I'm fine." "Bullshit. Let's go." He takes the picture from her hand but she grabs it back, "No! I-I want to investigate this further." He looks at her, "Fine." When they are on the front porch, he calls in to the station, "This is Snell. Look, I need a new sweep of the Sloane house. Yep, fingerprints, everything. Especially pictures of the tunnel and his hiding spots. *Everything.*" He hangs up. He leads Franklin back to the car when his phone rings again, "Snell. What's up chief? We're on our way back now. Out." He drives off.

"What's up?" "My package has arrived." He says as he lights a cigarette.

The floor plans of the main building at Santa Rita is displayed for all to see. Sloane has photos attached with arrows showing where the targets are going to be at at the time of their "resignation". He looks at his men, each one looking at the massive plan and each one plotting their own escape routes until the boss starts, "Okay, this is our target as you know. I want Xavier, Charlie to go in and disable the guards. Loche, you go in and get intel and any files. No excitement, understand? This mission runs silent until me and J. come in or if it goes to hell." He looks at them, "Questions?" "Yeah, while we is in there, what're you and Jack gonna be doin?" "We're going to be providing escape routes here, here and here." He circles rooms and windows for emphasis. "The backup plan is that everybody gets it and we blow up the building. The only signal I'm giving is the minutes you got left to get your ass out of there before it goes. Capice?" "Yeah." Loche responds.

Hours earlier, a military car pulls up to the building and out emerges Cassidy. He looks toward MT. Alitan and smiles. His cigar is placed in its favorite place, between his teeth. As he walks toward the doors, an armed guard stops him. He looks at the hand and then at the guard, "Boy, you better remove your hand quickly." He says in perfect Chinese, "I'm here to see General Ngoy. He's expecting me." The other guard radios in. After a few seconds, he nods and Cassidy continues his walk. He looks at the walls and decor, "Not bad." Cigar smoke trails behind him. Once inside the elevator, he taps ashes onto the floor. When the floor is reached, he proceeds toward a suite in the corner of the floor. Two very large men in deep blue suits and dark shades block large red doors. When he gets closer, they open the doors and he proceeds inside. "Hello my friend" the general says, smiling his yellow teeth at Cassidy. They hug and the general motions to a seat, "What brings you here? Checking on our meeting for your government's slice of their pie?" He asks as he sips on tea, "Not really Dray. I came to warn you of an assassination attempt on you and your meeting." "No doubt ordered by your government! I know your tricks Cassidy! Kill me and put in puppet leader so your country can still control Guam and Asia as well!" He laughs. Cassidy just puffs on his cigar, "Not really Dray. Although I do know where they are located right now. Plotting to take you out." He rises from his seat and pulls back the curtain to show Mt. Alitan. "Right there."

The general looks out toward the mountain and then at Cassidy, "Hmph. You are lying. Why would you tell me this? It is obvious you have ulterior motives..." "Damn skippy Dray. I want to be the main facilitator for

your consortium. And give 'Uncle Sam' his percentage cut for tax purposes."
The general thinks for a second, "You make sure everything goes right for
this meeting and I will ensure your place with me." "Fine." and they shake
hands.

   "How are you feeling G?" "Pretty good. My side stopped hurting.
How long have you been doing this?" "Oh, about a few years now. Being an
outlaw is pretty tough nowadays with that damn GPS and microwave tracing
systems, but I got it handled." Fonzo sips on his drink. "How long have you
and Marcia..." "Been together? I guess when I got confined to this chair
with wheels--" a cough interrupts him mid-sentence, "But we get along
okay." "Do you love her?" "Yes I do. But I figure it was the wrong place
and time. Oh well, maybe next lifetime perhaps." Fonzo laughs as Sloane
looks at him, amazed at his resiliency. "What's up?" Sloane's eyes goes
misty and he rubs his hand over his face, "I still miss her. Her laugh, her
touch. Her breath upon my neck when we're sleeping. The gentle caress of
her hands when they ran through my hair.." Fonzo lays his hand upon
Sloane's shoulder, "She was a good woman. I miss her too. I'm sorry we
didn't stay in touch more often." "Yeah, me too." A voice calls them
downstairs. "C'mon, got something you're gonna need for public exposure."
And Sloane looks at Fonzo quizzingly.

   When they arrive in the basement portion of Fonzo's brownstone,
Sloane sees various faces and designs on the walls. To his left, is a
computer screen with a 3D model of his face. "What is all this?" "Your
disguises, g. If you're gonna go out into the world, you have to hide your
face--you TV star you." Fonzo replies with a smirk. "Honestly, I was going
to go out in plain sight, since we all look alike anyhow." Sloane retorts back.
Cassidy rings his speed-dialer, "F.E.M.A. main desk, how may I help you?"
"This is Special Operations Organization Director Derek Cassidy, give me
your field ops leader-now." "Y-Yes sir, one moment." He is put on hold.
Two seconds a voice comes on line, "Peterson here, sir." "Mr. Peterson, no
doubt you have seen and heard the reports of Mr. Sloane, correct?" "Yes
sir." "I need a team of some of your best men. Sharpshooters, unarmed
combatants...a team of fifteen of your most skilled." "I'll have a list for you
by the end of today sir." "Thank you Peterson, goodbye." and he cuts the
connection; turns to view the scenic majesty of the Washington Monument
and casually glances at the board which has the faces of his target and
possible allies. The phone rings, "Yes." "Sir, its Steinbaker. Mr. Alphonse
Tracy is dead." "Are you sure?" "Yes sir, viewed the death certificate and
the grave sir at Arlington." "Any family?" "Just a widow sir. A Mrs. Marcia
Bengtson-Tracy." "Is she any threat to the operation?" "Negative sir."
"Make sure, Steinbaker. Check her thoroughly; she might know where our
mouse is." "Yes sir." Cassidy blows out the smoke and watches the birds fly
past his window.

"All we've got between us and Santa Rita is dense jungle. Possibly some guerrilla soldiers, but not likely. It looks like mostly farmers and jungle. But be careful. Our pickup spot is Umatac Bay. That's a day, two day hike from here; with opposition, it could take longer. Our objective is to do this job and get home in one piece. No heroics; no Rambo shit. If you meet opposition, keep it silent and attack at night. That's our way and it always worked --" an explosion shakes the camp where the Black Razors are meeting, "Who the fuck?" Loche goes as he gathers his weapon, a 9mm Beretta Model 12 submachine-gun, while Sloane gets his 9mm Beretta Model 12S. Jackson readies and aims his 7.62mm M60E3 machine-gun. Xavier Roberts dives under some dense foliage and aims his 9mm Star Z84 submachine gun and waits. His eyes surveying the area open to them. Charles Downing loads the 5.56mm Heckler & Koch MP53 and keeps the flash suppressor close by for mobile attacking. Smoke can be seen from their positions. There are no sounds to be heard anywhere. Sloane looks for Downing and Roberts and signals them to go scout the area for snipers. He orders Loche to search for mines or traps. He mumbles in protest then he is gone.

Jackson edges his way back to Sloane's position, "Who the hell is it?" "Beats me J. But whomever it is, shouldn't have known about us at all." "You don't think..." "I know its him. We're going to the backup plan immediately." "Roger." Downing returns, "We got company. Various men from Guam's new military, some from Anderson and a few unknowns. What's the plan?" "Backup plan." Jackson replies. Suddenly, a severed head rolls into view. It is a young Guamanian soldier; the blood is still seeping out from under his neck. Shortly, a little maniacal giggle is heard and appears Loche, with the young soldiers blood smeared on his face like war paint. "Got the little shit." He licks his knife, "What's the plan? Everybody's dying?" "You got it Jeri." Sloane says coldly, "Where's Roberts?" "On the west side of that field unit--waiting on us to make the first move." "Let's not keep the man waiting." The rumble in the jungle begins.

-Ports of Entry and Escape

Their feet climb the two story building staircase with a sense of indispensability. When the two homicide detectives reach their desks, the chief calls them to his office. Snell is the first to ask, "What's up chief?" Lt. Williams tosses him his 'package'. and then sits on the edge of his desk, "As of 0700 this morning, you two are off the case." "WHAT?!? Bullshit Lt. its my case. Who got it?" "Feds, Snell." He kicks the door and slams his 'package' down on the Lt.'s coffee table. Franklin looks at both men, "But sir, why? We were just starting to formulate some leads, then this?!?" "That's the way it goes. Orders came down this morning, from up top. The Commissioner says to stay out of it." "Damn Cassidy! I know its him. Chief, you gotta let us continue this--give us more time! We can nail that sonofabitch!!" "No, Snell! I already told you before, I don't want any accusations of impeding an investigation!! The order came from up top." "Fuck up top!" Snell screams, "I've been bustin my ass for this department for a long time; the least it can do is give me a few more hours to do what I gotta do!" Lt. Williams looks at Snell, who is fuming mad and ready to explode. Franklin is sitting in the couch, her head in her hands. The Lt. looks at them, sighs and shakes his head, "You got 48 hours to find me something. That's all I'm giving you cowboy." Snell picks up his 'package' and exits the office, "Thank you, sir."

Once they reach his desk, he opens his file drawer and pulls out all of the information he has on Sloane, "C'mon. We're gone." "Where we going?" Franklin asks, "To a quiet spot."

The jungle area is quiet. Gunfire sounds have not been heard in the last two minutes. Sloane and his team creep through the jungle. He gives Loche a signal. He nods and is up a tree going from branch to branch like Tarzan. Sloane signals positions for flanking and target acquisition, his men take the point. He crouches and duck walks toward the area simultaneously swinging his Beretta back and forth with his sights aligned. He hears feet running in the brush. Nimbly, he ducks and rolls behind a tree trunk and unsheathes his knife. When his quarry is close he sticks out his leg and trips him. He falls and loses his weapon; Sloane is on him in seconds whispering, "How many and where are they?" The soldier gropes and reaches for his fallen weapon, Sloane puts the point of the knife at his neck, "One more time: how many and where?" The man's eyes go wide and he stutters out, "3-3-30 in all...a-a click up to the east. Y-You will never make it off the island." "Who said so?" "T-The Federal guy." The soldier tries to throw Sloane off of him, but inadvertently allows the knife to pierce his neck and he dies quickly. Sloane gathers his weapon and ammo and continues onward. Then gunfire fills the air.

As he nears the hot zone, explosions ring in the sky followed by screams. He spots his men entrenched behind a building and returning fire. He comes in shooting the newly acquired M16 machine gun with reversible clip. Sloane screams like a wild animal as his eyes witness bodies hitting the ground. From the corner of his eyes, he sees Loche severing another head from its body; putting a live grenade in its mouth and pitching it back at their enemies. When a Guamainian soldier catches it, it immediately explodes, sending him all over the jungle. Jackson comes from behind the cover of the building and fires his M60E3, just waving it from side to side and the multiple rounds searing anyone foolish enough to be caught in its path. He smiles a big grin. Sounds of Loche's laughter echo throughout the battleground.

Sloane barks an order to Roberts and Downing, "Take out the building! No survivors!!" They go. Jackson joins with Sloane at a gathering of trees and reloads, "Some static huh? What's next boss?" Sloane looks around the damage, "Cassidy."

Screams of fear ring out from the jungle then silence. Loche emerges from the bush with two heads in tow. His body covered in blood, "Enjoyed yourself?" Sloane asks, "Yup. Tasty." he replies as he once again licks the knife. "Burn the bodies."

And Sloane walks toward the targeted building at Santa Rita.

Xavier Roberts peers through the binoculars while Charles Downing prepares the LAWS rocket. "Hey, take a look who's at the party." he goes to Downing as he hands off the binoculars, "Oh shit! Its--" "Cassidy. I know, he dies too." Sloane says coldly. Roberts looks at him with concern, "But Mike, he ain't in the plan..." "He dies too! He knew about our position and tried to get us killed by that small unit out there. I'm sick of him: he's history." Downing just nods his head and raises the launcher and adjusts his sights, "All ready boss." "Fire at will." Sloane tells him just as Jackson and Loche reach their position.

Downing fires and the rocket is off. It goes through the front doors and explodes inside the main lobby. Cassidy is surprised and runs to the nearest window, looking for the originating point of the explosion. When he draws back the curtains, a flash of sunlight shines in the distance, "Shit! They've survived the attack. Dray, we're gone--now!!" He drags the General and draws his weapon as the guards go ahead of them. When they reach the elevators, another explosion rocks the floor beneath them, "They're trying to take out the whole building! Those cocksuckers!! This way!" and they run toward the end of the building as screams permeate the first two floors and the intended targets rush down the stairs to escape the attack.

The windows burst open furiously and a rope ladder made out of bed sheets fall alongside the wall as an escape route for the dignitaries. When two of them reach the ground, Downing splatters their insides all over the grass. Roberts delivers two grenades to the others, followed by a screaming explosion for a response. Loche climbs up another side of the building and enters from a deserted office. He exits into the large hallway to hearing screams and orders in Chinese, Vietnamese, and other Asian languages. He creeps toward them, unsheathing more little blades and giggling to himself. Two men come around the corner running, he tosses two knives and they go down. Jackson scopes the grounds in the rear of the building, as the rear garage doors open and a black limousine races out. He quickly turns and fires rounds off. Seeing that the vehicle is bulletproof, he braces himself for the impact and goes over the hood, landing on his leg--breaking it. He screams in agony.

Sloane, seeing the vehicle racing away, takes Downing's LAWS rocket launcher and aims. His fingers squeeze the handle and pauses on the firing button. His eyes follow the limo. Just as the front of the vehicle nears the road, he fires. The rocket impacts with the rear window and exterminates the entire cabin. The doors get blown off from the explosion and the vehicle itself, flips and crashes on the road it was heading for. He drops the spent launcher and double times it back to the building. His ears picks up screams and explosions as he gets closer. As he clears the hill, he sees Cassidy running through the jungle, "J. I'm going after Cassidy." "R-Roger, meet you at the site." Jackson responds through the pain. Sloane races through the brush to catch his prey. His eyes dart everywhere for any sign of his colors or foliage movement. He unsheathes his 9mm Beretta and continues.

Clearing the jungle, Cassidy radios to the pickup chopper, "This is Bald Eagle, repeat this is Bald Eagle. I need a pickup immediately! The mission's been compromised. Repeat: the mission's been compromised!" "**CASSIDY**!!" Sloane yells as he finishes his distress call. He stops at the sound of his own name. Cassidy turns slowly while his good hand begins to draw the weapon which is hidden behind his jacket. Sloane cautiously steps towards him, "Don't pull it, Derek." A smile creases his face and he unsheathes it; Sloane pulls the trigger. The round meets the shoulder at the collarbone as Cassidy's arms brings the 9mm handgun up to fire. He screams and falls to the wet, mossy grass--his weapon still in his grip. As he tries to raise it up to fire, Sloane's wet, black boot smashes against the hand and pistol grip and keeps it down while his is pointed right at Cassidy's eye, "Go ahead...shoot."

Sloane cocks back the hammer, "All I want to know is why." Cassidy laughs, "Because you was expendable. Don't you get it? Your usefulness was up, Mike old buddy! We're two sides of the same coin son. You, are a methodical killer--" "Bullshit! I-We was given orders--" "Orders? Come on Mike! You, the whole team was the gun and I'm the scope. You, you was the best son! Saw that shit back in 'Nam. I picked you-all of you; you are the best except for that psycho nigga--" "Loche." Cassidy laughs again, "Yep. A pit bull that nigga is; gotta keep a leash on that one." "So you was gonna sacrifice the rest of us and keep him as your personal guard dog?" "Something like that." Cassidy responds coldly.

"Get up." Sloane hauls Cassidy to his feet. "Where we going Mike?" He drags him to a cliff. The rocks below are wet from the waves crashing against them. Sloane backs away from Cassidy, his 9mm Beretta still pointed at his head, "Anything else you want to say?" "As a matter of fact, yes." Cassidy eyes locks with Sloanes', "This isn't over Mike. Not by a long shot! Everyone's expendable; but me!" He laughs a ghoulish laugh as Sloane pumps ten rounds into his chest. Cassidy 'dances' as the rounds penetrate then he falls over the edge; his scream echoes over the waves. As

Sloane turns to leave, a spear comes flying through the trees and hits him in the leg. As he goes down from the impact, a machine gun butt clocks him in the back of his head; knocking him out.

Back at the building, Loche has placed and set the C-4 explosives with the mercury switches all over the remains of the building. Jackson sits on the grass, his leg wrapped in bandages and fastened with a splint to keep it immobile. His weapon sits in his hands; the tripod attachment rests on his good leg. Downing appears from the bush with a lit cigarette, "The General's dead along with a few of the other meeting members." Just then Roberts returns, breathing heavily, "No sign of the boss J. Think Cassidy's..." "Hell no. Cassidy's no match for Mike. We gotta find him. And get me some medical attention fast!"

The key enters the lock and turns it. The lock creaks in agony and futile resistance. The broad shoulder angrily bashes the door, forcing the lock to give. "Excuse the slight mess, the 'maid' is on vacation." Snell tells Franklin. When she enters the apartment, she sees pictures and framed photos of Snell in his early days in the police force. His living room is sparse except for a large coffee table which is littered with magazines and junk mail. "Have a seat. Cold brew in the fridge." He goes as he heads toward the rear of his home. "Were you married?" she asks, "A long time ago kid. Divorced me right after I came back from Nam. Called me a baby killer and shit; fuckin bitch." He chews on a straw then slides into a recliner. He rolls up his sleeves and breaks open the 'package' he received that morning.

"You see kid, I knew Sloane back in the war..." "Does the LT. know?" He shrugs, "Maybe. Who gives a shit. He was a good man; a good leader. I want that sonofabitch Cassidy and we need ol' Mike Sloane alive to get him." "What does the package say? Anything about what Sloane has on Cassidy?" Snell looks through the papers and spies news clippings of plots about secret testings of a biochemical agent unleashed on the public. Story about a secret faction broken up in Guam a few years ago. Then his eye catches the Post-It note attached to the clipping, "Holy shit." "What?" Franklin goes as she looks up from the files she has in her lap.

The note lists all of the active participants in the skirmish in Guam and the reason they were there.

Count on support of the people

His eyes throb. His head feels like a thoroughbred horse used it for bucking practice. His jaw hurts. He moves his tongue inside to check for loose teeth, he grimaces in pain, "Fuck." The room is damp, dark and musty. The brick wall is cold against his bare back. His wrists burn as he tries to work the shackles; the blood flows down his arm and falls toward the floor. The sweat falls down his entire body. Squeaks and scurrying sounds ring in his ears. Suddenly, the sound of keys opening a lock come into play. The heavy door creaks and writhes in protest. Light floods the room. Sloane squints as his vision adjusts to the new sensation. He spies two men: one big and tall, a heavy bone breaker; and a small to medium sized soldier type, give orders and asks questions. Sloane clears his throat, "Could one of you get me the manager of this establishment? I have some complaints that I need to share..."

The big heavy hurls his meaty fist deep into Sloane's midsection.

"So who am I gonna be, Will Smith?" Fonzo laughs, "Nah, you'll be even more inconspicuous. Just wait one moment..." His fingers dance on the keyboard and soon a face appears from the machine. The steam rolling off it like a sauna. "Your new face."

The big heavy smiles a big yellow tooth smile at Sloane. With one good eye, Sloane notices his gold tooth. As he begins to speak, another punch hits his jaw. The short soldier guy commands the big heavy to stop. His military boots clap across the stone floor as he nears his prisoner, "Tell me what you know yankee dog, we kill you quick. You no talk, we kill you slow." "I-I'm just a tourist here on vacation..." The blade cuts his left breast deep. His teeth clench so as to not to scream from the pain. He feels the heat of the blade going all the way towards his abdominal section, "Okay! I-I'll tell you anything..." Sloane goes through the pain. The blood flows down his legs; his feet slide on the puddles. "Then tell us what you were doing there at Santa Rita! Your body will feed our dogs. Talk!!" The big heavy leers forward as Sloane looks up. He sees the meaty fist raise up and drawn back, then released and he catches it. The big bruiser looks astonished at Sloane, who tries to smile but just knife jabs him in the throat, pulling out his esophagus. The soldier stands transfixed at the sight before him. He lunges the bloody knife at Sloanes heart, but it enters his own instead.

As he slumps to a pile of skin at Sloane's feet, his hands search for keys to free him. Luckily finding a set on the soldier, his feet shackles fall to the floor as does he. Gasping for breath and energy, he reaches for the knife and tears the shirt off the bruiser, wrapping it around his wounds and stepping towards the door. He looks around the area and sees guerrilla soldiers milling about. The door opens slowly and he darts towards a tent nearby and crouches for cover. His eyes scout the area and the sky. "Nighttime? How long have I been out?" he thinks to himself but is cut off as footsteps approach. His body tenses for the strike, knife ready and bloody.

"This is our best lead yet!" Snell goes and flicks the Post-it note at Franklin. When she reads it, she sees the names of the members who made up the team of the Black Razors. She grabs the files that Snell was looking through and comes upon the entry for the mission in Guam. "This was their last "mission" with Cassidy. Says here he was to have died when the building raid was in progress..." "We both know that's bullshit. Somehow that hardass survived and now runs one of the most powerful government agencies in the world. He gonna come off his mountaintop soon. Real soon. We've just gotta find Mike Sloane and keep him alive." "What if he doesn't want to go with your plan? What then Snell?" "I'll arrest his ass for manslaughter and destruction of government property and anything else I feel like at the time!"

The guards go down with a whimper between them. He puts the clothes on and grabs the weapons and walks, keeping his head down and shoulders slumped. When a guerrilla calls out to him he looks for an instant and waves him off, continuing on his path. When the guerrilla nears him, Sloane shoves the knife deep into his heart and pulls it up through his chest. He runs and jumps into a truck and sets two grenades and runs again towards a communications tent. When the truck explodes, he steps into the tent and immediately fires at everyone inside. When the clips run dry, he picks up another weapon and continues firing, taking out four to five men in one pass. Some of the guerrillas try to disarm him but he breaks their arms and then breaks their necks, leaving them lifeless, broken husks of skin and bones. His knife, maiming and searing flesh from bone, presents screams of agony and pain. The blood on his face cakes to a dry brittle substance, similar to a leaf in the fall. Screams echo inside his ears. Everywhere he turns his gaze, someone dies. When he turns finally to view the decimated camp, which is now enflamed and occupied by the dead, he takes a breath and turns and walks into the jungle. One thought goes through his mind:

Time to go home.

When the face has cooled and Marcia has helped Sloane put it on and arranged everything just right, He looks in the mirror and nearly faints, "You've made me white!!" "Yep, no one would suspect you to go around as a white guy. Look, I got you a plane ticket for California, Xavier and Charlie are gonna meet you there." "I haven't seen them in years, how will I know?" "Believe me Mike, you'll know."

Michael R. Sloane looks in the mirror one more time, and shrugs his shoulders, "Well," he starts, "At least the cops won't bother me." "I'll send you all of the intel when you get there. Those two nuts will give you the hardware that you would need. Good hunting."

"The hunt's only begun." Sloane replies.

End of Book Three.

NOW Available!!

A new comic book series for African-American readers!

MICHAEL R. SLOANE is a new action/adventure six-issue series by creator Adalberto McFarlane, which is sure to please those of you who just read the "Walking Through the Bell of the Beast" story in this very book! This is a 10-page prologue to the forthcoming series!

This series is not for children!

$2.00 plus tax (if applicable) and shipping and handling

For all you music lovers!! We have the *SLOANE – The Compilation Album!* This album presents various genres of music such as: Rap, Spoken Word, Rock, Freestyle Rap, and Instrumentals to name a few. Every track is an independent artist giving their all.

Radio friendly and anyone can enjoy it!

$12.99 plus tax (if applicable) and shipping and handling

To purchase these items, just log onto:

http://www.ninenappy.com/marketplace.htm

ENJOY!!